THE OCCASIONAL VIRGIN

THE OCCASIONAL VIRGIN

Hanan Al-Shaykh

Translated from the Arabic by
Catherine Cobham

PANTHEON BOOKS, NEW YORK

English language translation copyright © 2018 by Catherine Cobham

This work is adapted from two separate books originally published in Lebanon as *Imraatan Ala Shate Al-Bahr* (*Two Women by the Sea*) by Dar al-Adab, Beirut, in 2003, copyright © 2003 by Hanan Al-Shaykh, and *Azara Londonistan* (*The Virgin of Londonistan*) by Dar al-Adab, Beirut, in 2015, copyright © 2015 by Hanan Al-Shaykh. Copyright © 2018 by Hanan Al-Shaykh.

Library of Congress Cataloging-in-Publication Data
Names: Shaykh, Ḥanān, author. Cobham, Catherine, translator. Shaykh, Ḥanān. Imra'atān 'alā shāṭi' al-baḥr. English. Shaykh, Ḥanān. 'Adhārá Lundunistān. English.
Title: The occasional virgin : Hanan al-Shaykh ; translated by Catherine Cobham.
Description: First American edition. New York : Pantheon Books, 2018. Consists of the English translation of two Arabic works previously published separately under the titles: Imra'atān 'alā shāṭi' al-baḥr (2003) and 'Adhārá Lundunistān (2015).
Identifiers: LCCN 2017059865. ISBN 9781524747510 (hardcover : alk. paper). ISBN 9781524747527 (ebook)
Classification: LCC PJ7862.H356 A2 2018. DDC 892.7/36—dc22.
LC record available at lccn.loc.gov/2017059865.

www.pantheonbooks.com

Jacket image: *Woman in a Boat* by T. S. Harris. Private Collection/ Bridgeman Images.
Jacket design by Kelly Blair
Printed in the United States of America
First American Edition
2 4 6 8 9 7 5 3 1

For Freya

PART ONE

Two Women by the Sea

To reach the sea, Huda and Yvonne travel like a pair of ants, one behind the other. Two very cautious ants, as the road twists and turns deceptively, and motorists are surprised by the sudden appearance of people on foot, and by overhanging branches, extending in all directions.

'Let's cross over to the pavement,' Yvonne begs Huda, trying to free her hair from a trailing branch.

They stop for a moment, then set off on their way again, the never-ending stream of cars moving so quickly that their passengers hardly have time to turn their heads and glance fleetingly at the two women, who are in fact extremely pretty. One dark, one fair; one tall, one average height; both perfectly in tune with the summer weather: yellow shorts, barely skimming the top of the thighs, a short blue skirt with white polka dots, white T-shirts, and trainers so light and airy they almost lift them clear of the asphalt.

'Are we going the right way?' asks Yvonne, clearly anxious.

'According to the map ...' Huda answers, wishing that her friend would have second thoughts about going to the sea, as she had washed her hair the day before yesterday in preparation for the trip. This hair-washing involved an elaborate process of applying oil and allowing it to soak in, then washing it, spreading shea butter on it – which felt disgusting – and then rinsing, applying conditioner, wrapping each strand around rollers and sitting under a dryer, then brushing out each strand using a hand dryer. After this, she no longer had curly hair; instead it hung straight down over her shoulders, shiny as an aubergine.

They go off on a footpath, which rises steeply. Huge overhanging trees, and houses, or rather villas, apparently empty, surrounded by neglected gardens, black figs spattered on the asphalt, olive trees and dozens of squashes like orange footballs bearing no relation to the soft green plants which produced them. They turn on to a road with high walls on either side, and when there is no sign of the sea, Huda is filled with doubt. She examines the map and is not reassured. They follow the road to the end, and the minute they take another turn, on to a narrow track, they suddenly see the blue line on the horizon. Unable to suppress her delight, Yvonne begins running towards the sea, while Huda follows, worried and apprehensive. But getting to the sea is not as easy as it looks. High rocks, trees, stones and crashing waves stand guard over it. Have they come the wrong way? In their confusion they fail to notice the gap in the wall until a man rides up on his motorbike, dismounts, and climbs through it. Cautiously they follow and find themselves in a rock garden perched right on the seafront. The tension suddenly vanishes from Huda's mind as she stands confronted by white rocks like huge cacti. In the middle of one rock, that has a flattened top, yellow plants grow, the colour and texture of Yvonne's hair. Every time the water attacks them, the plants float briefly, then become still and smooth again. Huda secretly envies Yvonne's hair. They stand together contemplating these plants in surprise.

'They're like a woman's pubic hair,' says Yvonne.

'Is yours platinum blonde?' Huda asks. The rocks are otherworldly and she feels an overwhelming desire to walk on them, especially when she notices a young man and woman strolling over them quite casually.

'Let's go on those rocks.'

'No. Let's choose a place to sit,' Yvonne answers at once.

She walks over the red earth, where there are pine trees growing. Huda notices the resin dripping from one tree. They descend along a small path, just a few steps from the sea, and find nature has mixed sea and shore together. Patches of blue water surge between the rocks, with a single outlet connecting them to the wider sea.

Delighted, Huda breathes freely again. 'It would be difficult to swim here,' she says. 'Impossible, in fact. Never mind, we can sunbathe and sleep.'

'You must be crazy! We'll swim over the stones and seaweed till we get there.' Yvonne gestures vaguely with her hand, and Huda understands that 'there' means the open sea, just water and gentle waves, not like here on the shore, where it crashes against the rocks, white foam flying, raging.

'I've got a book ... you go and swim.'

'Are you joking? Did madam come all the way from Toronto and me from London so we could read? I don't think so. I've got jelly shoes that are great for swimming. You could walk over anything in them.'

Huda chooses a place under the trees but Yvonne wants to sit right beside the sea, in the sun, away from the trees and rocks. They spread out the towels. Yvonne strips down to her bikini, reaches out a hand to help Huda, who is slow to take off her skirt, claiming the zip is stuck. 'You go first. Anyway I want to climb on the rocks before I swim.'

Yvonne races towards the sea, stumbles on pebbles and sharp stones, scrapes her leg, but is unconcerned. She throws herself into the waves and swims, striking out in the water as if to confirm that she is actually there, in the Mediterranean, the only real sea as far as she is concerned. She wants to bite the water, hold it in her teeth, such is her desire for it. She dives like a duck, rediscovering its intimate spaces, a visitor after a long absence, savouring the taste of it, the coldness, the saltiness, the silence. Then she stretches one arm out on the surface of the water like a cat, then the other, swimming fast now, so that the sea can't escape from her, drinking in the air, embracing the water and exhaling, no longer seeing anything but the colour blue mixing the sky and sea together. She closes her eyes as if she has finally come home after a long journey.

Huda climbs back up to the pine trees, having refastened her skirt around her waist. She sees the tree that is oozing resin and smiles at the old familiar smell, the smell of the Beirut pine forest, and her grandmother bending over to light a fire with the needles and urging her to breathe in the smoke to cure her whooping cough. Huda continues walking over the rocks, which have become a proper footpath, bounded on either side by a metal handrail, so fine as to be almost invisible, a winding, uneven path, but broad enough. Crabs scurry from one hiding place to another. Small fish like eyebrow tweezers discover they are almost on dry land and escape back into the water. Huda looks for Yvonne and sees that she is still in the sea, which appears normal from a distance, no longer a theatre of horrors, a sea jungle, as it was when she saw it earlier.

She follows the rock walk to what is apparently the end, as her path is blocked by a sign saying '*Strada privata. Divieto di transito.*' An attractive young man leaning against a big iron gate and sketching a tree at bewildering speed looks at her and smiles. She smiles back at him, then returns the way she came, to the seashore where she can see her things waiting for her in the distance. A barking dog greets her. She ignores it and takes her place on the towel and the dog barks louder. The Italian family sitting nearby tries to quieten it down, in vain, as it continues barking at her, seeming to sense that she is afraid of it, even though it's tied to a chair leg. She removes her skirt finally and puts on the jelly sandals, intending to go into the sea, ignoring the big pebbles and jutting rocks. Everything is urging her to do it: Yvonne, who keeps calling her, the Italian family and their dog, the other bathers, and most of all herself. She makes several efforts to rush into the sea and swim out over the seaweed and pebbles, assuring herself that the water is only a few inches deep, but she does so hesitantly, so that the waves push her this way and that against the rocks.

Everyone must be looking at her, even the seagull, angry at the bathers preventing it from fishing. Yvonne calls her again, louder this time, laughing, and Huda lowers herself gradually in, holding her breath, waggling all her limbs in order to keep afloat, like a centipede trying to swim. Her head, clad in a bathing cap, around which she has wrapped a gaily coloured scarf, bobs up and down as she treads water, and she looks attentively around her, ignoring Yvonne's calls, studying the sea and sky. When she can no longer see Yvonne out of the corner of her eye, her heart begins to thump. Yvonne must have dived underwater hoping to surprise her. The thought of this spoils her concentration and she suppresses a cry and plants her feet on the seabed. Yvonne is lying on her back in the sea as if she is at home in bed. Huda takes a breath for the first time and dares herself to swim just a short distance, not far enough to get out of her depth. She continues holding her breath, thrusting her legs down from time to time, making sure her feet can still touch the bottom, then exhaling at length. *Yvonne can't have failed to notice how useless I am in the water*, she thinks. She splashes around noisily, lying on her back, the only position that doesn't make her look as if she is running away from a fire.

The water seems heavy, or maybe it's her head, heavy with fear of the water. She decides to get out, but Yvonne is swimming towards her, calling her back, so Huda increases her speed, pretending to be completely at ease in the sea, turning on to her back again, although in fact one foot is constantly testing to make sure the ground is still there, ready to receive her feet if necessary.

'Are you deaf? I've called you hundreds of times. You seem to like swimming in kids' pee.'

'I'm thirsty.' Huda changes the subject.

'And I'm hungry.'

Getting out of the sea is harder than getting in. Huda tries to look confident but finds herself colliding with rocks, toppled by waves each time she regains her balance. Yvonne laughs, but Huda doesn't join in, afraid she'll lose her balance again, until in the end she resorts to going down on all fours.

They finally reach their spot and eat apples, pears and KitKats.

'Will you climb those rocks with me?' Yvonne points to where several young men are standing, laughing, looking down at the sea and daring one another to jump in.

'Me? Are you crazy?' Huda hides her delight at the fact that Yvonne hasn't noticed she can't swim. *Why don't I tell her the truth? But I'm scared she'll insist on teaching me!*

'Come anyway. You don't have to dive with me!'

'Yvonne, you must be joking. Those rocks are really high. Don't be stupid.'

'In Lebanon I used to dive from higher rocks than those. Honestly.'

Yvonne walks quickly towards the rocks, which are shaped like wild horses, some of them dull black and eroded like old teeth. She bounds up them like a goat, and when she reaches the boys doesn't immediately dive in, but stands talking to them and looking down at the sea. *She must be scared,* thinks Huda. *Did she really climb up there to dive, or because she wants to get to know them?* Yesterday night before she went to her room Yvonne had said to her, 'I have a feeling I'm going to fall in love on this holiday,' and Huda had thought to herself, *Good luck with finding somebody who will love you back.*

Time passes and Yvonne is still talking to the boys and looking down as if inspecting the sea. Huda begins to worry that one of them might push her in as a joke. Then, all of a sudden, Yvonne dives off the cliff, her body a white trail left by an aircraft in the blue sky. She hits the water, then surfaces laughing.

Huda no longer watches Yvonne, who is climbing back up the rocks. Instead she gets to her feet and heads for the grove of pine trees growing in red earth, looking for shade. Its relative coolness restores her composure and the sea is blue now, unconfined, washing gently against the trees and touching the horizon. Gradually she feels calmer.

The sea is land with water on it. She will supply her own confidence. She is the only one who can teach herself to swim, not the others who have reached out their hands to help, one after another, encircling her waist as if they thought they were her lifebelts. To her their arms were like snakes, colder than the water, more unstable, less predictable.

The sea had depressed Huda ever since she was a school-girl, bent eagerly over a drawing of a Phoenician princess walking with her prince beside the sea, while their dog played with a shell. The creature that lived in the shell had dyed the dog's mouth a purple colour that clashed with the blue sea. She had written below the picture, 'The colour purple was discovered in the city of Tyre. Tyre is a Phoenician city situated on the Mediterranean Sea, like Beirut.' Then she took her crayons and gave the prince and princess the most beautiful clothes, and coloured the world around them like rainbows mingling with the blue of the sea, but instead of being happy that she had finished her homework, she felt a pain, different from when she had a toothache or grazed her knee: it began in her throat and descended into her belly, because the world and the colours she had drawn on the sheet of paper were what she longed for, unlike her house, empty of colour and pictures and music. The pain attacked her throat and she felt as if she was suffocating because she would never walk by the sea like this prince and princess and their dog, never set eyes on its blueness or the lovely colours of the prince and princess's clothes except in her dreams, and only then if she dreamt in colour and not in black and white as usual.

One day, Huda went up to the roof to find out if Beirut really was a Phoenician city on the Mediterranean Sea, but all she could see were low buildings with neglected gardens, a single high building sprayed with patches of red stucco, neighbours chatting on roof terraces and balconies now that evening had come, doves flying around and alighting at random, and a couple of cats darting away when they spied the neighbour woman pummelling a piece of meat with a wooden mallet, then returning to meow full-throatedly once she had finished extracting the thin white veins from the meat.

The sea must be somewhere in Beirut: she drew it with a blue crayon in her geography book. She learnt how to colour the sea so it appeared like a real blue surface, shaving off fragments of a blue crayon with a razor blade and rubbing them on to the page with a piece of cloth. The sea was always to the left and she wrote above it in a sloping hand 'The Mediterranean Sea', a phrase as vast as the ocean.

Huda's first encounter with the sea happened when all of Beirut rushed to look at an Italian steamship that had run aground on the beach. Among the crowds that day were the people of Huda's quarter, old and young. They all dismounted from the bus and ran together across a sand that was like burghul wheat, and a little boy pointed to it and asked his mother if it was an enormous garden of tabbouleh. Huda reached out her hand incredulously to touch the sea; she saw the ship, like a big black bird with one wing stuck in the sand and the other lying on the surface of the water, exposed to the sun and rain.

She couldn't remember if she had paddled in the water that day or not, although she did remember the women's legs with their protruding veins, and their heels so dry and cracked they looked as if they'd been cut with a knife. She tried to picture her mother's legs, but couldn't, for she had rarely seen them without thick black stockings. The first time she had taken off her dress and put on a swim-suit, she had thought of her mother's black stockings and headscarf, but these images vanished as she looked down at herself and thought, *Is this really me?* She remembered hurrying into the water, into the roofed-in sea, the place known as 'The Women's Swimming Pool', constructed of three walls and a fourth with an opening halfway along to let the seawater in. She found out by chance that the girls of her neighbourhood went to the women's swimming pool with one of their aunts every Sunday. In tears, she reproached her best friend for not telling her of these excursions: 'So the sea's not for people like me?' Her friend, also in tears by then, answered that they didn't dare take her with them because they were scared of her parents, which upset Huda even more, as she realised she would never be able to escape the fact that her father was a religious man, something that would slam doors in her face whatever she tried to do in life.

Her friend was well aware that Huda was the most open-minded of all the girls: she knew Arabic and French songs by heart and told jokes and imitated film stars and people in their neighbourhood, first and foremost her own mother and father, and in the end Huda joined the rest of them at the pool. Of course, there was no need to warn her to keep it secret, as everybody knew that her parents would not only punish their daughter but also the friend's aunt who had brought them, and their fury would extend to the other parents, for swimming in the sea was forbidden for girls like her, even in this covered pool. The sea meant wearing swimming suits, which meant that a girl's reputation was soiled like a silver bowl whose gleaming surface had become tarnished and blackened.

Once the rumour got around that the girls from this traditional quarter were going swimming in the sea, explaining that it was the women's swimming pool they were going to did nothing to diminish the scandal. The pool was on the other side of the city, the more modern and open side, where there were nightclubs, European show-girls and foreign business men. Women paraded about in high heels and sandals revealing toenails painted in vivid reds, as they dragged their dogs along, dogs with full bellies who only growled when inferior people walked by. Going to the sea, even if it was to the women's swimming pool, meant walking through streets lined with hotels and book-shops that displayed foreign magazines with women's faces and bodies on their covers and sold fiction and new novels about love, passion and betrayal. The inhabitants of these quarters looked different from Huda's neighbours: their shopping bags were filled not only with meat and vegeta-bles, but also with strange imported fruit; they didn't walk as if the cares of the world were on their shoulders; and they even went to eat in restaurants, undeterred by the cost, although their homes were close by.

As the bus drove the girls to the women's swimming pool, Huda wished all the passengers knew she was going to the sea. If only she were carrying a straw basket with her own swimsuit in it instead of wearing this borrowed one under her clothes.

The moment the bus heading for Ras Beirut crossed Burj Square it started filling up with students from the American University and surrounding schools. Huda studied their different clothes, especially their white socks, and wished she could wear the same. They wore tennis shoes, the likes of which Huda had never seen before. She tried in vain to catch the eye of a student carrying a tennis racquet, and swore to herself that she would finish her studies at the American University. The bus stopped among beautiful buildings and the aunt descended only after she had made sure that all six girls were on the pave-ment. They passed by mixed beaches and all kinds of hotels and came to a halt where a blast of noise was emanating from an entrance with no door or sign. The ground was wet and as Huda followed the other girls she saw the place was plunged in semi-darkness, and there was a woman with a cigarette in her hand whose brown breasts showed beneath her unbuttoned blouse, for all the world like a child's bottom. The woman held out her hand to the aunt to take the entrance money she had collected from the six girls in the bus, then asked if any of them needed to borrow a swimming suit. She lit another cigarette as they all hurried to the small changing room, which was also dark, and from there out to the covered pool, where the noise of the waves competed with the noise of the bathers.

Huda descended the few steps where the water came in from under the wooden balcony and broke in waves on the rock in the middle of the pool. Could this really be the sea? The water crashed against the walls, and she wanted to escape out into the open sea away from the children and their mothers and grandmothers and the woman with red sores all over her body like hibiscus flowers with yellow pus on them. Another woman was wearing a baggy swimsuit, revealing pubic hair that reminded Huda of the brown whiskers on a corncob.

The eyes of the five other girls from her neighbourhood were fixed on Huda's skinny body, as she stood there without her voluminous skirt, four pairs of knickers and two cotton vests, alone with the nicknames she was known by locally: Umm Sa'dallah, after the famous old woman of their quarter, who was over a hundred years old and whose body had shrivelled and creased like a pleated skirt; Bone Soup; and Kibbeh on a Skewer. But her best friend quickly rescued her from this humiliation, taking her enthusiastically by the hand, and Huda submitted, abandoning herself to the water, which began to spill over her, leaving behind specks of salt soft as dew where it touched her. She saw her body under the water, brown, hairless. The water washed her feet clean from the black shoes she had been wearing that day. Her mother always dyed her white shoes black in winter and so far hadn't bought her any new white ones. The water made her light as she clung to a rock, wrapping itself around her as it pleased. Archimedes was right then. She was floating. She felt she owned something: her body was a gift, not created merely to fulfil certain functions. It wanted to play, so she played with it, floating, turning round in circles, splashing happily like those around her, while mothers scooped up water as if they were picking fruit and sprinkled it over their children's heads.

Nobody made any attempt to swim. Mothers shouted at their children to be careful they didn't drown. The sea was treacherous. The sea was the sea wherever it was, even imprisoned in this room. Even if it only reached your waist. Even if big black car tyres encircled the bathers' bodies like lifebelts. The water was not blue, not azure. How Huda used to love that adjective: the azure sea. And the word 'Venezuela'. And 'ocean'. And laughed at the word *albasifiki*, because as well as the Pacific Ocean, it could mean in Arabic 'You're wearing my knickers.' The water had no colour. She took hold of it. It wasn't white. Why do they call the Mediterranean the White Sea? The water was there and not there. It was the first giant, or was it the second? She could no longer remember what she had learnt in her reading book about the two giants, water and fire. Water was like candy floss: the more you had the more you wanted. They all came out of the women's swim-ming pool with their features somehow clearer, brighter. The aunt seized hold of Huda's plaits and said thank God they're not wet, and Huda answered that she'd thought of that and pinned them on top of her head before she went in the water.

Four years passed before Huda immersed herself in the real sea – she was sixteen by then. She walked on the white sand and lay on a bright towel in another borrowed swimming costume, while European pop songs thudded in the air and she thought about boys and dancing to noisy music. She was afraid of lying in the sun for long, didn't want to get caught. But it was the sun that ultimately exposed her, or rather the lack of sun turning the salty water in her rolled-up towel and swimsuit into a foul odour after she came back from the beach. She carried them around from place to place, like a scorpion carrying its young on its back, thinking she would spread them out to dry on the communal roof terrace, but she was afraid her neighbours would report her to her parents. What if she dried them on the balcony of the neighbour on the other side, though? The one who liked reading and would understand? No, her husband raised pigeons that might soil the borrowed suit. Days went by without them being dried and they began to stink. Yet only Huda's mother smelt them, as she was used to sniffing out the food that Huda's grandmother persisted in hiding under beds and in cupboards until it went rotten.

When her mother finally caught her, Huda defended herself, denying that she'd ever been to the beach or worn a swimsuit in public, insisting that she'd only had it on at her friend Salwa's house, whose bathroom contained a big bathtub, 'so we float around in it as if we're at the seaside, because you won't let us go there. We're trying to be like other girls – like other people.' But her mother was ready for her: 'What about the sand in the folds of the bathing suit? Look! Here's the proof. See the sand, the little shells?' Huda had collected them and wrapped them in a sheet of newspaper, but denied that the sand and shells were an indication of any wrongdoing, and shouted at the top of her voice: 'Obviously we scatter some shells and sand in the bottom of the bath, so that we feel as if we're really in the sea, since you won't let us be like other people. In any case, I don't understand why you're so angry. Especially since my father loves the sea. Didn't he tell the woman who cried black tears to go to the sea and swim, even if the waves were high?'

Huda remembered this woman who came to her father with her eyes outlined with kohl to make them look bigger, and when Huda's mother offered her tea, black tears ran down her cheeks and she muttered, 'Our Master's fatwa will decide whether I live or die.' Huda's mother comforted her: 'Think good thoughts, sister, and put your trust in God.' This woman had come from the far south of Lebanon, from Naqoura, to ask for a ruling from the shaykh, intending to follow his instructions. She would never agree to let the bean-seller mount her, even if that meant he killed her. She wanted to choose another man. Huda only understood as time went by that 'mounting', the word the woman used, meant having sex like a mule. The first husband of the woman with black tears, who had divorced her three times, was not permitted to return to her until she had slept with a second lawful husband for one night and he had divorced her in the morning. The woman dried her tears, took a deep breath and said in a voice that the whole house could hear, 'Master, I can't bear to let the bean-seller come near me, so how can he be my husband for a night? He gives off such a stink of onion and garlic that I can't breathe.'

Huda's father nodded sympathetically, saying, 'Cleanliness is part of our law. The Prophet (praise be upon him) used to say, "Make sure you are well dressed whenever you go to the mosque," and he refrained from eating onion and garlic before he went to pray.'

Huda's father looked distracted and stared at the ceiling before arriving at a strange fatwa to solve this woman's problem. Still staring at the ceiling he said, 'You come from Naqoura, don't you? Now, my question is, can you swim?' The woman looked embarrassed and hesitated before replying, thinking perhaps that he was going to tell her to take the bean-seller to the sea to wash all traces of the foul smells off him in the salty water. She answered that she was a good swimmer, so he said to her, 'Go with your sisters or female relatives to the sea and expose yourself to the powerful waves and the spray so that they enter you, like a lawful husband entering you, then you can return to your first husband.' A strange fatwa, as if her father considered the attack of the raging sea on the woman equivalent to sex. Was he being wise here, was his understanding of religion modern, or inspired, or even based on medical knowledge, or could it be that he was just a realist, wishing to avoid complications! And the sea was masculine, of course. She wondered if this was his way of interpreting the saying 'Religion is there to make things easier, not harder'; then again maybe he was simply being pragmatic, irresponsible even.

This lie about Salwa's bathtub did not stop her father from striking his face and weeping. Shaking his head and looking skywards, he mumbled: 'My daughter clothes herself in depravity and exposes her body to men. Where shall I turn my face, I a man of religion, who shows others the way? Where shall I direct my prayers? How can I stand by and let my beloved daughter perish in hellfire?' Meanwhile Huda's mother wore even more black after this event, prayed more often, spoke in hushed tones and no longer addressed a word to her.

*

A young man hovering nearby brings her back to the present. He reminds her of someone she's met, his face is familiar and he's approaching with a smile. Most of the men she has known have admired her body, starting with the first boy in her life, on the beach in Beirut. His gaze had forced her to wrap a towel round her, even though she was wearing a one-piece then, unlike now as she stood facing this Italian in her bikini.

'Would you like to swim at the villa's private beach?' he asks her first in Italian, then in French and finally in English, pointing down the rocky path, and she remembers he is the artist who was sketching a pine tree at amazing speed. She hadn't recognised him at first because now he is only wearing trunks and has a straw hat on his head. Before she can answer, he adds, 'You can have a walk in the gardens too. I look after them.'

'I thought you were an artist.'

'I'm a landscape architect. I'm responsible for the trees and plants in this area ... The villa's gardens are famous and its private beach isn't rocky or stony.'

'Thanks, but I'm waiting for my friend.' Huda points over towards the rocks.

'Ask her to come too. I'm working at the villa all day. Actually, I'm living there for the time being.'

'I'll ask her, thanks.'

'You must be on holiday ...'

Perhaps if they weren't both in their bathing suits, this would be going more naturally, she thinks. *They don't know whether to look at each other's bodies, or into the distance.*

'I wish! This place is so dear to me. I've spent the best summer holidays of my life here with my boyfriend. I'm just here for a couple of days this time.'

Then her eyes fill with tears and she turns her face away from him, sensing his embarrassment. Although she's looking down at the ground, she hears him whispering, 'Try to come, please. I'll be waiting for the two of you.'

Yvonne, as she dives for the fourth time, has to outshine the boys, who stand there astonished by her energy and daring. When she examines the water, it is with eagerness and excitement, not hesitation or anxiety. She takes a deep breath, tenses her body for the dive, and plunges into the sea, which is dark for a moment, then luminous and transparent as she opens her eyes underwater. As usual when she dives and manages not to drown, then shoots back to the surface like a yo-yo, she thinks it's a miracle, like the Virgin Mary giving birth to the Messiah.

The boys ask her where she's from, since she's obviously not from around here even though her hair's naturally blonde. It's as if she is too beautiful to be climbing rocks like these and challenging them to dive from the other side, which is higher and rises to a sharp point.

'I'm from Lebanon, from the north. I was born by the sea.' Yvonne answers their questions happily, full of confidence, studying the boys one by one, like her uncle who used to go around the towns and villages searching for the meanest birds for the cockfights he organised in their local town square. Old and young would bet on these birds with what little cash they had. Of course she's looking for the most attractive one now, not the meanest. They are younger than her, only students, but she is more daring. She was born in a house whose windows all looked out to sea – or did the sea look in at them? As a child, Yvonne didn't believe that there were cities like Beirut and Tripoli with shops and cinemas, couldn't picture a vast area where aircraft took off and landed, or mountain tops covered in snow. The sea was the world. The changing seasons came from the sea. She discovered the existence of strange animals like seals. She saw death there when the sea cast up bodies on the shore. Yvonne ate from the sea. She witnessed magic the first time she saw the fish her father had caught coming out of the oven with its flesh transformed into soft, succulent matter falling off its big bones in the roasting tin. Even the people's expressions came from the sea: 'I love you a whole sea'; 'We have a sea of rice'; 'He's very smart: he can take you to the sea and bring you back thirsty'. Their swing was an old boat slung between two trees.

The sea washed over her bed, too, nestled in her thoughts. She heard the roar of the sea all the time, but as soon as she slept, it slept too, only waking when she awoke. As the house opened its eyes, the questions began: What's the sea like today? Stormy or calm? Rainy or sunny? Like a mirror? Like oil? What shall we eat today? Sea urchins? Whitebait? Or shall we shovel the wet sand into little mounds and sieve out the cockle shells from it?

But learning to swim was what confirmed her existence. As soon as her father sensed she was ready to swim, he told her to move her arms and legs as powerfully as she could, assuring her he would keep his hand under her stomach at all times. She relaxed and struck out in the water with all her might, forgot about his hand and found she was floating. She held her breath as he instructed her, for ten seconds, twenty seconds, becoming an expert in controlling the activity on which her life depended. She put a stone on her stomach so as not to rise up in the water. She imagined the water filling her ears and over-flowing into the back of her nose, and when she felt the need to breathe again she was sure the water had filled the space behind her nose and had no alternative but to go up into her brain, making her feel so light she was flying.

She never tired of this feeling. She began to discover many secrets from her swimming. The sea was like a school: the pupil had to move up from one class to another. Being content with swimming and holding your breath for a few seconds would be like staying in the same class year after year.

Diving was what all the children of the neighbourhood, children of the sea, aspired to. They used to form pyramids, standing on each other's shoulders and taking it in turns to jump, and the moment Yvonne reached the top she would plunge into the sea. One day her mother bought her a bathing suit composed of panties plus a bra, not just panties like the younger ones had. 'Because your chest is bursting out,' she said. Like eggs being cracked open before they are thrown into the frying pan and the oil splutters and the liquid turns white and frothy. Her chest was like two eggs, growing bigger all the time. That day, Yvonne didn't want to climb on to somebody else's shoulders and throw herself into the water. She wanted to dive from a rock like her three brothers. Her desire to do this was so great that it outweighed her passion for the cheese and cucumber sandwiches that her mother brought to the beach, wearing a straw hat, trousers and a long-sleeved blouse, as she liked neither sun nor sea nor sand.

Yvonne rushed to find her brothers: 'I want to learn to dive. I'm old enough now.' She stood looking at the water, regretting her decision, and would have changed her mind, but her mother's voice echoed in her head, scolding, sighing, complaining, ordering, and she was compelled to stare down at the water again, as if she was waiting for one of her brothers to push her in. In no time at all she was aware of her heels pointing skywards as she plunged downwards into a dark chamber and, invigorated, shot back to the surface like a bubble in fizzy water. She became so addicted to diving that when she had her injections against typhoid, TB and smallpox at school and was told she couldn't go in the sea, she believed she had discovered the true meaning of despair. All the same, she left the house, went down the hill, past olive trees, thorn bushes, rocks and thyme, wearing those plastic jelly shoes to protect her from the sharp stones, and sat on the rocks and imagined the dark room she entered whenever she dived from a height, and the way her head would break free from it in response to a magnetic force that brought her happily to the surface again.

By the third time she dived she was confident, able to think clearly. Imagining the resentment she felt towards her mother vanishing into the sea, she told herself that from now on she wouldn't protest when she was asked to help with the housework, or lose her temper every time her mother spoilt her brothers, or shout at them to come and help their mother too. She would even agree that the perfume from the orange trees outside the tiny bathroom window mixed with the steam and made you dizzy, as her mother maintained.

The new light blue swimsuit that her mother bought for her because of her breasts 'bursting out' inspired her to rush one early morning to the rock that was forbidden to all but her big brother. She stood on the forbidden rock for more than five minutes, looking at the calm water. It called to her until she threw herself in, shouting, 'My brother Tanius, my brother Tanius.' This time she went down until she almost touched the bottom. She understood why this rock was forbidden. The higher the spot you dived from, the deeper you went, unable to see anything but seaweed, water and silence. Her attempt to rise to the surface from the very bottom of the sea was the test that would prove she was confident, had complete control over her breathing and all the related parts of her body – nose, throat, feet, hands, eyes – in short, that she had become an expert swimmer and diver. And so it happened: she found herself rising up and up until she reached the surface, then she swam to the shore and ran home, shouting, 'I dived from the high one!' She woke up the household, relating what she had done, indifferent to the slaps and blows that greeted her news, although the pinches her mother gave her made her believe in the existence of fishes that were poisonous despite looking beautiful.

'Are you trying to kill me, make me wear black for you?' screamed her mother, but even so Yvonne didn't think she really cared about her. That day, Yvonne saw her mother's true colours: she only loved the boys. When one of Yvonne's brothers was ill, her mother would put vinegar compresses on his forehead to draw out the fever, muttering, 'May Jesus reach out his hands to heal you. May the Virgin Mary intercede for you. May I die if it will make you better.' She sang the praises of their male members and her favourite anecdote was about planting a kiss on Tanius's little willy, only to have the scallywag pee in her mouth.

It would be one thing if she'd slapped Yvonne across the face in spontaneous anger, but her pinches were hard and deep, designed to get a good handful of flesh, to reach right down to the bone. She pinched her face, her arm, twisted her nose, but her fury and resentment remained unquenched, so she grabbed hold of Yvonne's hand and pulled her along, and when Yvonne resisted and sank to her knees, she continued dragging her over the floor like a heavy rag. She shoved her into the bathroom, locked the door and sat outside, with her back against the door. This went on for hours, and Yvonne could hear her mother inhaling hard on the mouthpiece of the narghile. She could picture the water swirling in the glass base of the pipe, and waited in vain for the gurgling sound to soothe her. Finally her mother asked her, 'So, have you learnt your lesson?' as if hoping Yvonne would say no. 'Don't ever dive from the forbidden rocks again.' 'I swear by the Virgin, that's the first and last time,' replied Yvonne, bursting into tears. But her mother was in no hurry to open the door, and carried on accusing Yvonne of things she didn't understand: 'You've humiliated your eldest brother. Destroyed him. Castrated him. I pray to God you can never have children.'

Everybody in the neighbourhood came to know of her dive from the forbidden rocks, and the children followed her around as if she was the Pied Piper of Hamelin, begging her to teach them how to dive. Her brothers, especially Tanius, were delighted when she began asking them technical questions, once she had decided she would search for jewellery when she dived, like Dumb Jibran who spent his life looking for a bracelet that had belonged to a relative of King Farouk of Egypt. She wanted to find something that would make her rich, so the family would raise her high on their shoulders in celebration. But all she found were the hiding places of silvery fish that rarely looked like jewels. She searched at length for oysters, opening dozens and never finding a pearl. *She should take more time*, Yvonne thought, *and not open them for several weeks – be content with observing them from a distance, swimming as silently as the fish in case she disturbed the creature in the shell and prevented it from making a pearl.*

But she stopped examining oysters, stopped diving in the sea, when their house began to roar like the waves, even in calm weather; its walls crowded in on her, as the bombs of the civil war fell haphazardly and Dushkas rained fire on them. She and her family were finally forced to take shelter in the ice factory, where everyone cried and shivered in the frosty chill, trying to keep away from the walls that protected the ice from melting and absorbed its coldness. As she listened to the adults talking about wars and what was going to happen next, she wished they could be like the Vikings and hijack ships and roam the oceans. Ever since she had first seen pictures of the Vikings, she had been convinced that they and not the Phoenicians were her forefathers, and was enchanted with them. The men were like her father and the women like her mother: blonde hair, light eyes, pale pink skin, deep red lips that were soft and cracked like the ivory handle on the big spoon.

She chose the Vikings as her special subject in history class, and when the teacher asked, 'Why? What about the Phoenicians? They were extremely advanced, and their name is mentioned in the Old Testament,' she answered, 'The Phoenicians had brown faces, and I'm blonde like the Viking women.' She didn't add that she was tough and hardy like them, or that she had a small nose unlike the Phoenicians, or that like the Vikings she loved travelling the wide ocean as if she was riding a horse, and loved their low ships with their dragon prows and ribbed bellies like skeletons, or dinosaurs lying on their backs. The Vikings took their women with them on their travels, especially when they settled in a country, while the Phoenicians crossed the seas without their women, trading cedar wood and pine, purple dye and blue glass for gold, musk and monkeys.

She was sixteen years old when she first heard people screaming in fear at the destruction and savagery of war and she couldn't believe how impervious the sea remained, ebbing and flowing as usual; how the birds alighted on it, taking off and vanishing high in the sky the moment they heard a shot. While old women beseeched the Messiah to come now, this minute, Yvonne prayed to the Vikings, wherever they were, to rush to their aid. But identifying with the Vikings turned out to be a disaster, for now the war came to confirm her conjectures about them in unexpected ways: their descendants practised savagery, killing, abduction, occupation of whole areas, while the Phoenicians' interests had been confined to matching this colour with that and carrying exquisitely embroidered cloth to harbours all round the world.

The sea had not left its traces on the people of her town, except on their arms and faces, tanned over many years by the sun's salty rays, which provided them with warmth as they shivered with fear in the ice factory. She sat there cradling a cardboard box full of shells she had gathered and painted and everything else she had found while diving, including a broken piece of a dish, apparently from their area and not from China as Yvonne had believed. Her mother remembered the pattern and knew which family it came from – it was a fragment of a narghile, the part where the tobacco goes, maybe it's called a tobacco dish, made of glass. Yvonne sat in the ice factory, watching her mother crying silently as she waited for one of her sons, who had disappeared two nights before to join the fighting, or so they said. *If only my mother would rush to the sea like our neighbour,* Yvonne thought, *when her eight-year-old son disappeared and people said the sea had swallowed him. She plunged into the waves, unbuttoning her dress, taking out her enormous breast and trying to squeeze out a drop of milk, pressing on the nipple until she screamed in pain. And on the seventh day the sea spat out her son's body for her.*

Being able to dive into the water, even while she was sitting in the ice factory, relieved Yvonne of the tedium of the long hours of waiting, fed her and kept her warm. As she brought her shells close to her ear, she dived into the sea and felt safe there. She heard a shell complaining that it missed its mother and sisters, while her mother wept silently for her three boys, even though two of them were right in front of her, which was a miracle, since all the other young men of the area had gone off to the war, just as if they were setting off for work or school. She wept silently, as she did whenever she washed their clothes and rubbed the stains off their underpants with pride. Yvonne dived down into the sea's silent rooms with the keys to her larder, her school, her mind; then she returned to her seat, reassured, and looked round the faces of the local people, noticing Jamil, the boy she had allowed to kiss her two years before, after she had given up waiting for him to take her to the Afqa Cave, where Adonis kissed Aphrodite for the first time, and where the river flows red at the start of spring in memory of Adonis, killed by a wild boar's tusks.

Who's going to kiss her now, out of these three Italian boys? Yvonne studies them one by one and settles on Lucio, the most talkative, and even though he is a bit plump, she is held captive by his gaze. It is as if there is some strange collusion between his eyes and lips. Each time he looks at her, his lips move closer to her. He is peeling an orange and eating it greedily. She pretends to be busy looking at the water, then persuades herself it's best just to be the diving companion of all three. She asks them how high the rocks are, and if they always come to this particular spot. She doesn't ask them what their jobs are, in case she is asked the same question and is forced to tell them she owns an advertising company. Whether this makes them run away or hang around, she'll end up being rejected. It's happened so often before. She wonders if men sense she's going to stick to them like glue, and that now more than ever she wants the heat of that contact to result in her stomach swelling like dough in the oven. All the ones she's actually been in love with, she's lost: they've escaped, disappeared, melted away. All of those who wanted to stay were married, or twenty years older than her.

I'm going after this dive, so I'll say goodbye. Does she say it out loud, or to herself? She doesn't want to have expectations, realises she's probably ten years older than them. The sight of their skinny chests, tanned by the sun, almost hairless, their thighs like the thighs of three statues of David, their wet hair chaotic, reckless, free, gives her goosepimples. To her delight they all start shouting, either objecting to her leaving or saying goodbye. How is she supposed to understand these Italian signals and gestures? She dives in before she can regret her decision and to her great joy they throw themselves in after her and chase her, joking, surrounding her. *As if I'm a duck and they're my chicks.* But their boldness as they swim around her doesn't suggest they think of her as a mother.

Lucio accuses her of lying, and says there's no friend waiting for her on the beach by the rock walk. She asks him to swim with her to see for himself, but he replies by asking her to go back up the rocks with him. She likes the idea, but the sight of Huda in the distance makes her change her mind. She begins swimming faster towards her, thinking, *You don't say goodbye in the sea,* so she doesn't, and they don't.

Huda isn't reading a book, or swimming or sunbathing. *She must be waiting for me.* Yvonne feels a pang of guilt. She was the one who had convinced Huda that they should meet on the Italian Riviera instead of in Lebanon: 'It's hot and humid. And London's dead. I can't bear it in August.'

They had met two years before in Lebanon as guests of an organisation that invited some Lebanese women who had been successful abroad to give lectures and exchange views with students. Huda was a theatre director, Yvonne the owner of an advertising company.

Moments after they met, their friendship had taken root, and they became each other's lifebelts in a country that was beginning to be unfamiliar to them. They no longer knew the right note to strike in order to feel in harmony with it again, for they had left twenty years before, Huda via Syria and Yvonne in a Greek ship from the port of Jounieh. The two friends had agreed to take a short break before Huda began to direct her new play in Toronto. This play, an adaptation of *One Thousand and One Nights*, had dominated her thoughts since the idea for it had flashed into her mind a year before, so when Yvonne suggested they meet in Italy, Huda clapped her hands for joy. Her mind was in urgent need of a rest.

Yvonne throws herself down, panting, on the towel that Huda has rearranged. Everything in her is flushed except for her green eyes, which look almost blue, as if the sea has lent them its colour.

'Are you thirsty?' Huda senses Yvonne's embarrassment at having abandoned her.

'My mother wouldn't let us drink straight after swimming. She used to say, "The chest is dancing. When it calms down."'

'My mother always used to tell us the story of her relative, a traffic policeman, who dropped dead after he drank a pitcher of cold water straight after he came home "all hot and sweaty". A heart attack. They said his heart couldn't take the cold water in the height of summer.'

They laugh together at the Lebanese mentality. Neither thinks of saying, 'Christian or Muslim, we all do the same things'.

The breeze softens the ferocity of the sun. The smell of pine trees fills the air. They eat more fruit, drink from the Thermos.

'You're a champion swimmer! I don't know many Lebanese women who swim like you!'

'Really? I was raised by the sea. When I moved to London I was always looking to my left, expecting to see it! We left our town, the sea, our life there because of the fighting. The war was just like a nightmare, not real, as if the sea cancelled it out or made people forget and distracted them from what was happening on dry land. Even the boats that began carrying people to Cyprus looked like cruise ships. My departure for London was a tragicomedy. See, I'm using theatrical terms just for you! My middle brother hired a speedboat whose owner promised him he knew the Cyprus route like the back of his hand. After three hours sailing we were sure we'd reached Cyprus as we saw dry land and a man fishing. The speedboat owner talked to the fisherman in English and when he didn't answer, my brother butted in, in Arabic: "Why isn't the bastard saying anything?" So the man shouts in Arabic, in a Lebanese accent, "Why are you calling me a bastard? Just because I don't know English?" Then it became obvious to us that we'd been sailing around in Lebanese waters for three hours. So a week later I left on a Greek liner.'

'Well, I went from Beirut to Syria by car, then to Canada to join my brother who'd left Lebanon earlier in the war. I still remember the Syrian official who inspected my passport. He handed it back to me with a note inside it. It said, "I'm throwing myself on your mercy and asking you to help me get a visa once you're settled over there. I promise I won't cause you any trouble. I want to leave this country. I'm desperate to emigrate. Please, I beg you." As if he guessed what was going to happen in Syria. The poor man thought fleeing Syria was his ultimate solution, seemingly unaware that in leaving his country part of his soul, too, would be lost to him forever.'

'Do you think we're still unmarried because we live outside Lebanon? I mean because we've changed – because we aren't completely at home either with foreigners or Lebanese?'

'None of my female cousins are married and they've never left Beirut in their lives! There are no men there, the men are all working in the Gulf. By the way, I did find you a husband. He's a landscape architect. He asked if I wanted to go swimming at the big villa and have a look at the gardens,' Huda said.

'Really? I hope he was handsome!'

'Very, and he said I should bring you with me.'

'Did he see me?'

'I don't know, maybe.'

'Well, I found three husbands. We can train them ourselves, they're young and bad!'

'The ones you were jumping and diving with?'

'No. Different ones. I met them underwater. Like mermaids, but men.'

They laugh, and Yvonne wonders to herself how it is that Huda isn't married yet, even though Huda told her from the first day they met that she wasn't interested in marriage or children, but somehow Yvonne never believed her. She is so beautiful and tall and shapely, with firm muscles and a flat stomach. Men must be afraid of her body, smooth under her tight clothes, with not a trace of cellulite.

'Oh, Yvonne, I forgot to say that I told the landscape architect that I came here before with my boyfriend,' says Huda, adding, 'and it seems I believed my own lie, because the tears started pouring from my eyes.'

'Sometimes I don't understand you, Huda. Why all this drama? There's no need for it.'

'Maybe I didn't want to tell him that the sea had taken me back to the past. I really don't know!'

Of course I know, thinks Huda to herself. *As far back as I can remember I've used lies and tricks as weapons. When I was fifteen I pretended to the son of the woman who owned the shop by the bus stop that Amal, the neighbours' daughter, had fallen in love with him. I gave him a love letter that I'd written myself and he answered it straight away, asking Amal to meet him before his mother came to take over in the shop at ten. Then he began expressing his love to her, even though he didn't know her, but said he'd fallen under the spell of her words and her beautiful handwriting. When I delivered her tenth letter, where I promised to meet him, as I'd done in every letter, 'so that I could caress his blond hair and cover him with passionate kisses and cling to him like a magnet to metal', the boy fell on me, holding me, kissing me, forcing his tongue between my teeth, squeezing my breasts and stroking my neck, till I freed myself, frightening him with my screams and running off as he began undoing his flies. To this day I don't know if he'd guessed all along that there was no Amal and I was the one who loved him.*

And what about the time I pretended to a guy in Toronto that I had poor eyesight just because of an impulse to be close to him, intimate. It was early on a beautiful evening, everyone was hurrying to their homes, clubs, lovers, while I was a lonely owl hooting for a companion, and then I saw this handsome guy whistling Leonard Cohen's 'Hallelujah' as if he was telling the whole of Toronto, or whispering in my ear, that his melancholia was charming. I felt both cosy and excited, but instead of talking to him, I began feeling my way with my umbrella and only after a bit asked him to help me cross the road. When he took my elbow, I grabbed hold of his hand and didn't give it back until he announced that we'd arrived.

The rocks are still empty of the three boys and their laughter. Yvonne suggests they accept the eligible landscape architect's invitation.

'What about our things?'

'We can ask that family to look after them for us.'

Before Huda has agreed, Yvonne hurries to talk to the family in English and pet their dog – the same one that was barking at Huda earlier that day – and returns with a confident smile. They leave their two baskets with them and take the rocky path until they reach the dead end where the notice by the gate of the villa reads '*Strada privata. Divieto di transito.*' When there is no sign of the landscape architect, Huda is disappointed, despite having been afraid she would be forced to swim.

'What's his name, so we can call him?'

'I don't know.'

'Hallo. Hallo,' calls Yvonne at the top of her voice. Huda kicks her just as the man comes hurrying into view and opens the black wrought-iron gate for them. He shakes them both by the hand and introduces himself as Roberto.

'Do you have a favourite tree; if yes, do you hug it?' Yvonne asks. 'And can you choose a tree to be my husband, like they do somewhere in India?'

Roberto smiles and replies, 'I'll show you my work in these gardens,' and takes them to the point where they should begin their tour.

'When you come back I'll have finished work, so we can go for a swim.'

They walk around, feeling their disappointment at his curt reception melt away in the face of a beauty that is beyond words. A fountain, tall palm trees, chinchona trees with smooth bark whose leaves give off a captivating scent of quinine, jacarandas scattering their violet blooms on the ground, mimosas, lemon trees, white poplars, olive trees and others – whose names Huda doesn't know – that resemble vast umbrellas crowned by pink flowers like cotton wool. There are dwarf palms, more fountains, jasmine, honeysuckle, gardenia. Huda stands before a lily like the one in her neighbours' garden in Beirut, with white trumpet-like flowers. She moves closer and smells the same smell, thinking, *Why was I scared of these flowers?* then moves away from them and the memories of her father they have evoked. Yvonne calls her. She's standing transfixed before a pond, where there are ducks swimming, and large fish almost leaping into the air, mouths open, as they jostle one another to catch the red hornets buzzing over the surface of the water like helicopters.

The landscape architect appears and addresses a question to them, of which all they understand are the words 'big tree', then indicates to them that they should follow him as he goes down some steps and turns to his right. They come face to face with a giant olive tree, its roots like huge rocks, like an elephant's legs, and gasp simultaneously. The architect nods as if expecting this reaction, gesturing to them to follow him again and pointing to roots that have spread out and bored into the wall.

'How old is it?' asks Huda in English.

'A thousand years old, maybe. Where are you two from? Greece?'

'Lebanon. But we live abroad. Me in London and her in Canada.'

'You must be Christians. You speak English fluently.'

'I'm Muslim and she's Christian,' answers Huda.

'If only the guys in ISIS could see you in a swimsuit!' laughs the architect and they join in his laughter.

'I bet if the guys in ISIS could see her now, their faith would grow even greater and they'd say, "God is omnipotent indeed".' Yvonne declaims the final phrase in Arabic.

'Yvonne! I don't believe it. How do you know this saying?' exclaims Huda in astonishment, also reverting to Arabic.

'Why shouldn't I? London is an Arab city, and partly Muslim,' laughs Yvonne, then in English: 'When I ask the Egyptian doorman at the hotel where I swim each day if he can park my car near the entrance, and not in the garage, he says, "I'll try, God willing, for only God is omnipotent."'

Huda laughs and so does Roberto. Perhaps it will be really easy for him to choose between them now. *Will he choose Yvonne, because I'm a Muslim?* wonders Huda, surprised to find herself thinking in this way. But what about the Canadian she'd thought she was in love with, until he'd asked her in all seriousness if he had to convert to Islam if he wanted to kiss her? And the woman who came to her flat to measure the windows for new curtains and asked if the glass chandelier that hung at an angle was tilted to face Mecca? And the many who were convinced after 9/11 that she would understand its perpetrators and harbour at least a little admiration for them – those who were extremely diplomatic whenever the subject came up, until they heard Huda criticising them, and extremists in general, declaring that she didn't really believe in any religion.

Roberto says that his work in these gardens will be completed within months, as the villa and its surroundings have been donated to the government by the family who owned them and are to be opened to the public.

'As soon as I arrived here, I knew I'd found a hidden treasure, but working on it has made me prematurely grey.'

He bends his head, showing beautiful black hair with hardly a trace of grey. *He must know how attractive he is,* Yvonne thinks. She clasps one hand tightly in the other, afraid she will reach out involuntarily to stroke his hair.

Roberto suddenly takes Huda's hand in his and begins leading them down to the sea. Then he turns to Yvonne, offering her his other hand, and walks between them, dividing himself equally between the two women. As the sea comes into view, Huda knows Yvonne will capture his heart when he sees her plunging into the water and swimming like a mermaid, when he registers the deep green of her eyes and her blonde hair, smooth as silk, and her desirable, curvaceous body. Roberto asks them if they want to swim and Huda's tongue unexpectedly saves her: 'I'll sit in the shade. This is my first day at the sea.'

The three of them go down to the beach, which is surprisingly sandy, with not a rock or stone in sight. Yvonne charges into the sea in her usual way, discarding her shorts and T-shirt in a heap. She calls to Huda and Roberto to join her, saying how lovely the water is. Roberto looks at Huda and she doesn't know if he's asking her to accompany him or excusing himself. She indicates to him, looking at the sea, that the water is waiting for him and he nods his head understandingly. Roberto catches up with Yvonne. Huda hears their voices, their laughter. Why do people always laugh when they swim together?

Then, to her surprise, she sees Roberto emerging from the sea. Apparently Yvonne, the mermaid – whom she'd earlier watched pursuing the opposite sex as eagerly as a male dove, diving off the rocks so she could be with three boys much younger than her – wasn't able to lure him into her cave, a big white coral shell, surrounded by colourful fishes. Roberto tries to shake the water off him without much success, then sits down beside Huda and asks her what her name means. He confesses he has rarely been brave enough to approach a woman as boldly as he'd approached her that morning, and was so keen to get to know her that he'd left a business meeting with the intention of coming down to the sea for a swim, afraid she would leave like a lot of people do, as the swimming isn't easy in these waters. Voices rise in the air, calling, 'Yvonne! Yvonne!' The three boys are back throwing themselves off the rocks on the public beach.

'Yvonne dived off those rocks all morning.'

'I know. I watched you both from time to time. I was worried about your friend. I didn't realise she was such a good swimmer! And I was worried about you too, when I noticed you standing for so long on the sea walk holding on to the handrail. I had the feeling you were scared you might throw yourself into the sea without meaning to!'

She looks sad as it strikes her that this stranger seems to know her better than her own family.

'I've never been to Canada, nor even America,' he continues cheerfully, trying to lighten the mood again. 'How I envy people like you and Yvonne just taking the plane to Florence and then coming here for a day or two.'

'Sometimes I wish I'd never left Lebanon. Maybe it's better to be content with staying in one place, since if you leave you can't escape this feeling of schizophrenia, however balanced a person you are.'

'But you were escaping the war, weren't you?'

'No. A lot of people stayed. I left Lebanon because I'm a coward. I didn't have the courage to pursue a career in theatre with my family around.'

'You must be happy. You're lucky, you've seen the world. And I'm very happy to have met you.'

'Same here! Tell me, why do pine trees drop resin? I love the smell of it. We used to chew it when we were kids.'

Roberto takes her lips in his, which are like two salted almonds.

Yvonne swims with the three boys, desperately wanting to be alone with Lucio, without the other two, who only smile, laugh and comment on what Lucio is saying to Yvonne. He flirts with Yvonne, as if their presence emboldens him further, and tries to unfasten her bikini top. When he fails, he dives under the water and thrusts his head between her thighs. Yvonne laughs unrestrainedly, thinking his charm is a blessing from on high.

It is the sea that has generated these boys for her to have fun with, made her feel like flirting. The London cold imposes different sorts of encounters. The men melt away like sugar in a cup of hot tea and she always ends up regretting that she has radiated hope and given herself to them. How should she behave with Lucio, convinced as she is that appearing too keen will make her seem like a lonely old maid? She never knows whether to say yes or no, what to say at all, when to take the initiative.

Lucio finally manages to unfasten her bikini top, while his two friends stand at a distance like a pair of guardian angels. She lets out a scream, laughing as she catches sight of her breasts like two scoops of vanilla ice cream, then covers them with her hands and asks him to do up her bikini top again.

'Are you engaged or married?'

'Why?' Her heart beats faster. *He must have guessed that I'm over thirty-five from the look of my breasts.*

'This ring.' He bends his head to look at it.

'It's from Lourdes. You can see if you look carefully. The Virgin Mary on my finger. See her head and feet.'

'I don't believe it! Have you been to Lourdes? Are you like us?'

'I haven't been. A friend brought it back for me.' She doesn't tell him it brings luck, that she wears it to get a husband. 'What about you, do you have a steady girlfriend?'

'It depends on the situation. At the moment I'm trying to make you my steady girlfriend.' He laughs.

He must have a steady girlfriend. Yvonne reproaches herself for allowing herself to forget that he was just living his normal life before she and Huda descended on the beach, and would continue to do so after today.

What about her normal life? All she sees in her mind's eye are offices, hers and those of her employees, and her attempts to meet men, and gather ideas for advertisements.

One more glance at Lucio and she resolves to be off. How could this body, this being, these two beautiful rows of teeth ever be hers!

'I'll get sunburnt if I stay any longer. My friend must be waiting for me. I have to go.'

'We were getting ready to leave as well, but we suddenly saw you in the water again. Where were you hiding?'

She laughs, almost tells him that she looked for him and he wasn't on the rocks.

'My friend and I went to the big villa. The gardens are like paradise. And we swam from the private beach there.'

'How did you get in? I thought it was still closed to visitors. God, you must be important girls.'

They all come out of the sea, which continues to rise and fall, restless and calm in turn. She waits for Lucio to ask her something, but he doesn't. He's not in a position to invite her to dinner – after all, he's a student – but what about a coffee? He doesn't even ask her if she'll be at the beach tomorrow. He knows the hotel where she's staying, he says, after correcting her pronunciation of its name, adding that he's never been inside it.

She busies herself calling to Huda, who is sitting with Roberto next to the Italian family. Her heart, which has sunk like feet sinking into the sand, extricates itself when she hears Lucio saying, 'Will I see you tomorrow? Around noon. Promise?' She nods delightedly and finds herself leaning forward to kiss his cheek, at which he pulls her to him and plants a kiss on her jawbone, close to her neck. She continues walking over to Huda and notices Roberto heading towards the villa, raising a hand in greeting to her from a distance.

'So, it's been a day in paradise. What's going on, Huda, you wicked girl!'

'You were watching us, were you? And I watched you with the boys. They looked as if they were going to eat you up.'

The Italian family walk past, saying their goodbyes to Yvonne and Huda, but the dog stops and rubs his head against Yvonne's thighs like a cat. She bends down to stroke him, demanding a kiss, and he stands up on his hind legs, encouraged by the mother, who says, 'Oscar, *dalle un bacio*,' so he sticks out his tongue and licks Yvonne's face.

'That's disgusting,' remarks Huda.

'You seem jealous. Do you want the dog to kiss you too?'

Huda thinks they are about to leave the beach and Yvonne is going to ask her about Roberto, but Yvonne is in no hurry.

'Let's take our time. I've still got a packet of biscuits. Has Roberto gone back to work? Surely he invited you to dinner?'

'He asked me where I was staying and said he'd call me. What about you?'

'They're broke, those boys, but the one I like, who's called Lucio and studies medicine in Florence, is sweet and really funny. He's asked me to meet him tomorrow.'

'You mean we're coming back here tomorrow?'

'The boys said it's the best place. Anyway, Roberto will make you come back here whether you want to or not. Maybe he'll take us inside the villa.'

They drink water, wishing it was coffee, and devour the whole packet of biscuits. The sun is still there in the sky, but shining from a distance, its rays bestowing a gentler warmth. It's as if the sea has grown weary for the first time since the morning: its movement is more regular, and it looks like a piece of silk, blue, violet. Seagulls alight on its surface and as soon as they see a fisherman, they all head for him as if pulled along by nylon threads tied around their legs.

'I'm not tired of the sea yet. Let's go and swim again.'

'OK. Let's go.'

Huda gets to her feet, feeling a great sense of relief. The sea has emptied of bathers. Now she can try out anything she likes, so when tomorrow comes and Roberto invites her to the sea, she won't start to shake, and when darkness falls and she's with him on the beach, she won't get scared and try and run away, for the sea at night scares her as if it's trying to entice her by stretching out silently before her so it can pounce on her like a savage beast.

She runs to the sea and to her delight Yvonne decides not to go in with her.

'I want to dive from the rocks again.'

Huda goes into the sea. She resolves to put her head underwater.

I'll wash my hair at the hotel and put rollers in and straighten it again, she reassures herself, bringing her face nearer and nearer to the surface of the water. As soon as her nose comes into contact with it, the salt enters her throat and her whole face is in pain. She coughs violently, withdrawing her head, but the pain increases and the salt grows saltier. She has to take a deep breath and put her whole head under in one go, as the swimming teacher in Canada tried to show her, in a swimming pool where the overwhelming smell of chlorine paralysed her senses, and she could no longer remember what jasmine or gardenia or popcorn smelt like. She wanted to get out of the pool, tried to explain to the teacher how when she held her breath, it made her see outlandish images, produced by the remotest corners of her brain.

Now she is making for a semicircle of rocks, like a peninsula, knowing that she will certainly scrape her legs in the process, but continuing nevertheless, allowing herself to be pushed violently against the rocks by the water. She plants her feet more firmly on the bottom, willing her limbs to be strong. *I'm not going to let the water beat me. I'm going to get there. And when I'm there I'll put my head in the water and hold my breath and float. I'll swim with my head in the water and won't care what's beneath my feet. The water will hold me up.* She makes three attempts, not allowing her feet to touch the bottom, but after a few moments one foot goes into spasms and her toes curl up. Still she doesn't despair, but stands on one foot, rubbing the toes of the cramping foot to restore circulation.

She tries to swim again, to move forward a little way, even the length of her own arm, but everything in her seizes up suddenly. She returns to the shore, trying to work out what's wrong with her. Sadness rises like bile in her throat and bewilderment is an octopus extending its tentacles inside her head. *What shall I do?* repeats Huda to herself. *What shall I do?* She goes to find Yvonne, unable to bear the water for a moment longer.

She did not repent and stop going to the sea, in spite of her father's tears and her mother's silence, which lasted for months. She discovered from one summer to the next that the sea had many faces: it appeared in the secrecy of the women's swimming pool, in a private beach attached to a restaurant, or in the suburbs, where there were sandy beaches, stony beaches and big seawater pools for swimming, only a hair's breadth from the sea, but without the jellyfish that looked like tropical flowers swept into the ocean by the waves and discharged into the Mediterranean.

The sea has its rites and customs. It requires a variety of swimsuits, not one old one borrowed from a girl in some obscure neighbourhood, but a range of styles and colours. It requires straw hats, slender gold or silver bangles or anklets, creams and oils, supplied by friends and containing tincture of iodine, olive oil, vinegar, lemon juice, a mixture that Huda shook vigorously before applying it to her body and lying in the sun like a fish in a frying pan.

It was enough for her to enter the water, as if she had been thirsty for a lifetime, her body making a sound like the whisper of liquid extinguishing the flame on a cooker. It was enough for her to walk on the sand, the warm grains massaging her feet, getting in between her toes, enough for her to feel proud of her body, whose beauty was shown off at its best as she lay on a towel in her swimsuit: slender waist, long legs and a pretty back, while in her clothes she looked too skinny.

She was lucky to be naturally brown, not because these days there were songs on the radio extolling brown beauty, but because her visits to the sea would not be discovered. All the same, she took every precaution, wearing a long skirt over a short skirt, removing the long skirt and putting it in her bag in the hallway of an apartment building close to her house before she got in the taxi or bus, then putting it on again before she went back home, making sure not to forget the long-sleeved white blouse over her sleeveless top. She learnt not to remove her bathrobe before switching out the light, not to hug her pillow or wrap her arms around herself as usual, but to keep them straight down by her sides as if they were in splints, hands clasping her thighs, for fear her arms would reappear outside the cover. She didn't think about her face, and that's the place where the sun lands first in summer. Her brother would whisper suspiciously to her, 'Your face only goes that colour by the sea.' Defiantly she would answer that she sunbathed on the roof, exposing just her face, and did he want to stop her doing that as well, when she had already been forbidden to go to the women's swimming pool?

He tried to catch her out sometimes, helped by her mother who sneaked in and looked through her clothes, even smelling her shoes, while he made an effort to leave work at odd times of day, in the hope of surprising her on her way to the beach. Eventually he grew frustrated and gave up watching her: she was like one of those little lizards with eyes that move in all directions, allowing them to see their enemies, even if they are behind them. Until, one day when the summer was nearly over, taking with it the fun – the music coming from all around the beach, the daydreams in which she pictured a boy lying at her side and promised herself that next summer they would become a reality – she heard her name being broadcast

45

over the loudspeaker. She jumped to her feet from the sun lounger as she had seen other girls do, and walked unhurriedly to the reception, imitating their nonchalant air. How often in the past she had longed to be one of them, all conversation turning to her, all eyes upon her.

It must be her friend Salwa, Huda thought, *the only person who knew she was here.* She was probably contacting her either to say she couldn't make it or to confirm that Huda was at the beach, since the sun was taking its leave of the sea that day and there was a rain cloud preparing to burst the moment the swimmers stopped praying for it to hold off. But Huda was suddenly rooted to the spot, her heart in her clenched teeth. In front of her was her father, with their neighbours' son, a taciturn youth who never raised his eyes from the ground to look at her or any other girl.

She prayed the earth would open up and swallow her. She gasped, a deep intake of breath she hoped might be her last. She put her hands up to cover her chest and thighs. If only she could go blind, turn into a pillar of salt. Her father, in his black robe and green turban, had trusted the pious, dignified neighbours' son when he asked him to come along to the opening of a Shia technical school, only to find himself in surroundings he could never have imagined. Then, before he had a chance to ask what was going on, hearing his Huda's name over the loudspeaker, and seeing her, his daughter, but different.

Her father had struck his face, then buried it in his hands. The sound of his sobbing had risen until it was as loud as the waves. He swayed his head from side to side as if he was trying to save her from drowning before his eyes. If only she had been caught dancing or with her head uncovered, or with a boy – but to have been caught in a swimsuit in the water's embrace? Water, a source of sorrow as well as cleanliness and life in their house: 'a drop of water', 'the water's cut off', the word 'thirsty', they all reminded her parents of Ashura and the battle of Karbala, and here was Huda throwing herself not into a few drops of water, but into the whole big water, into the sea.

Yvonne does not head straight for the rocks as she intended, but finds herself walking into the water.

She proffers her lips to the sun, closing her eyes as if waiting for a kiss, examines herself in her swimsuit, its various shades of pink, and the bikini top exposing a large part of her breasts. She looks at her stomach, her navel with a gold stud in it where you might expect sand, the slight redness at the top of her legs caused by the salt water.

The sea seems to have put on a new suit of clothes in this spot, its colour blue and green now. When she was diving into it earlier, it was dark, indigo. She closes her eyes, picturing the water slapping against the rock, over and over again, always making the same sound, giving off spray. This excites her, and she finds herself swimming now like a knight on a young horse, undoing her bikini top, so her breasts go free in the water and she races after them, the bikini top attached to her wrist. Then she lets her hand move down below her belly and removes the bikini bottom, then rides the horse for a while before dismounting and lying on the surface of the water. The water pounding on the rocks pounds against her breasts, her navel and below her belly. She closes her eyes and surrenders to the water, letting it do what it pleases with her, moves further out, afraid someone will hear her moaning, then remains in the water for some time until she has become completely still and quiet. She has no desire to swim, wishing the water would carry her to the shore, relaxed from the pleasure. Inertia seizes her as it

47

always does after she climaxes on her own, and she doesn't want to think much. She hurries towards the high rocks again, and this time she is weeping as she dives, shouting, 'I've come back, I've come back,' and the waters of the Mediterranean carry her to her house in Lebanon. The waters wash her, as two women bend over her, like at the public baths, scrubbing her body with a loofah and soap, and when the colour of the water changes, Yvonne cries, 'Am I really that dirty?' Her arms are made of iron. Her blonde hair is the same as her older brother's, her trouser suit is Harris tweed, she carries a leather briefcase, wears shiny shoes and walks with a confident step.

The waters of the Mediterranean carry her to the steps of their house in her seaside town. She looks in through the windows, where the sun used to enter, despite her mother's best efforts, through cracks in the wooden shutters, making a shadow like a black question mark in the room. The paint is still fresh and green on the inside although it has faded outside, like the love between her mother and father; her father who had kidnapped her mother, Violette, when she was asleep in bed in her family home. Violette hadn't woken up until she was sitting beside him in the car. Was it conceivable that Violette would have remained asleep? Violette who was descended from stock that broke rocks with their bare hands, and whose mother said nothing when her husband dropped dead as they visited their land in Syria, just hurried to dress him in his best suit and tie, placed his hat squarely on his head, put him in the car and told their driver to go back to Lebanon, convincing the Syrian authorities at the border that he was asleep, dead drunk, cursing him, vowing she would ask for a divorce as soon as they reached Lebanon? All this to avoid paying death duties and being subjected to Syrian inheritance laws; as she explained to anyone who expressed surprise at her strength and shrewdness, 'Naturally, laws are a nuisance in death as well as in life.'

Violette, the bride kidnapped while she was sleeping, started to have regrets a few months after her marriage to the man her mother had refused to accept, because he was not the same class: he was a lawyer, not a feudal landowner like her family, 'So how will he understand the language we speak, which has been shaped by the land?'

Only a few months after the marriage, the bride Violette began repeating her mother's phrase, comparing her old life with her new one, often weeping as she did so. Only at night when everything was shrouded in darkness did she feel really happy, when it was time for her to have a glass of whisky and make love to her husband. She gave birth to three boys and two girls, cursing each time she had a girl. She forgot what a monthly period was, or what the tops of her legs looked like. She wanted boys that would replace her mother and brothers, who had never made their peace with her and had cast her out of their lives for good. She wanted boys who would succeed in restoring her pride, a beautiful lily that had bowed its neck and drooped prematurely.

Now everyone in the house rushed to greet Yvonne, taking her leather bag and suitcase from her, flinging the doors wide. Yvonne entered, hugging everyone, for she was the one who had left with a hundred dollars in her pocket and endured the hardship of working as nanny to a Lebanese family for years, then studied, worked hard and acquired her own company, raising her family to its previous status.

She sat, while they all hovered round her, competing with one another to talk to her and make her feel welcome. Her mother was preoccupied with making coffee and bringing sweets, piling up the food in front of Yvonne and trilling with joy. Her father's eyes filled with tears of delight, while her three brothers passed the time by biting their nails and shifting their watches or their genitalia from side to side, and rooting around in their ears with the nails of their little fingers, which they had left to grow, in order to distinguish themselves from the other peasants who ploughed and worked the land. The voice of Umm Kulthum still played, cigarette smoke rose in clouds and the shutters remained closed: the living room was unchanged; the television screen was alive and well and the dish of sliced carrots in its usual place as Yvonne's mother went to squeeze lemon juice over it.

'In the name of the Cross, in the name of the Cross,' murmured her mother, studying Yvonne as if she had forgotten her face, never braided her hair for her. She looked at her daughter's clothes and handbag, the rings, watch, bracelets, earrings. *I wonder if she travelled first class?* She felt a hot wave of anger tickling the back of her throat. *My daughter's selfish. Why doesn't she travel tourist class and give us the difference?*

She looked at her, thinking: *I used to sit like that, feeling pleased with myself, before I was married. I didn't give a damn! I wonder how such thin heels can bear the weight of her body?* Her eyes met Yvonne's and she was afraid her daughter would guess what she was thinking, so she said hurriedly, 'Glory be to God, you're the spitting image of my father. You sit just like him. If I put a pipe in your fingers, a black cloak round your shoulders and a felt cap on your head, you'd be him, I swear to God.'

Yvonne smiled at her in embarrassment, not believing a word, but knowing what her mother was getting at: *It's not surprising you look like your grandfather, because you've made a success of your life, while your brothers are still scrabbling about in the dirt trying to earn a living.*

Yvonne looked at her brothers, smiling as if apologising for her mother's harshness, and noticed they were jamming their fingernails even more energetically into their ears. Her mother did not continue, but Yvonne and everybody else in the room knew the monologue by heart: *Why did I pretend to be asleep and trust my fate to a young lawyer, even though there was every indication things wouldn't work out? For example, he was used to eating tabbouleh that consisted almost entirely of burghul wheat: you could count the bits of tomato on your fingers. That wasn't a trivial difference: their tabbouleh indicated weakness, a sense of failure, even in the people eating it and the dish it was served in, while the tabbouleh in our house filled our stomachs and we derived strength and confidence from every morsel we ate ... But why return to the wretched past, when I have my daughter Yvonne here briefly restoring my youth and energy, briefly of course, only briefly, as she's sure to marry soon and then she'll regard her husband and children as her family, not us. That's what always happens: my boys married but they're constantly in the house, around me, loyal to me and their father, while Yvonne's far away, and I only see my other daughter every couple of weeks now that she's married. I don't believe the boys are loyal to us because we still help them with money and make sure everything Yvonne sends us goes into their pockets, nor do I think they're waiting for us to die so they can divide the house between them, although that's what Yvonne claims, so does her sister, who repeats everything she hears. Both of them still accuse me of spoiling the boys. Maybe it's because I sent them to school with cushions, fearing for their bottoms on the hard wooden seats. Or because I was pleased with them when they were thrown out of school. I knew they were fighting for their rights, and if they could stand up to their teachers, they could stand up to the world.*

Unable to contain her nosiness, her mother got up and went over to Yvonne's suitcase, deliberately stumbling against it and taking hold of the label, to check whether Yvonne travelled first class, as she had heard.

I'll ask her tomorrow ... Perhaps if she grilled a fish for her and smothered it in tarator sauce, sent someone out to catch sea urchins for her and sprinkled them with salt, garlic and lemon juice. But she couldn't wait and found herself asking Yvonne, as she opened her suitcase, whether she had brought what she'd requested: 'a silk *robe de chambre* for your brother Tanius'. Yvonne rummaged intently through her luggage, bringing out various clothes that she held out to her mother, murmuring, 'For Tanius and the kids', but her mother didn't take the things from her and asked stubbornly: 'The silk *robe de chambre?*' at which Yvonne shouted that her son was a parasite and didn't deserve to wear silk.

Her mother put her hands on her hips and spouted all the resentment that had been accumulating inside her, like a camel that had forgotten how to regurgitate for a while, then remembered suddenly what it had to do: 'The fact he didn't succeed is all because of you. You're the one who humiliated him, in fact you humiliated all three of them. You wanted to compete with them, dive off the highest rocks, travel abroad. You're selfish. And they helped you humiliate them out of the goodness of their hearts, otherwise you'd be rotting away in this kitchen now.' Before her mother had finished and began dabbing at the spittle around her mouth, Yvonne heard again the sound of their house roaring like the waves, its walls seashells whose loud rumble hurt your ears when you listened to it. She hurried to take leave of her family, recalling what the teacher had told them about seashells: 'Spineless creatures that live in the water.' She left them on the first wave, plunging deeply beneath it, and the place where she dived crumbled in pieces, as if she had caused an earthquake. The waters of the Mediterranean groaned in pain, like a giraffe with backache.

They drag themselves back to the hotel in complete silence. Neither of them asks the other why are you so solemn, why so quiet, is anything wrong? Because they are both certain that spending the first day of the holiday on the beach ought to have refreshed their bodies, set them free, let their minds stretch out in a delicious, but temporary, stupor. And then each of them is trying to extract herself from the maelstrom of the past with a couple of simple questions: Do you think Roberto is married? Are we going to spend this evening alone in the hotel?

In the evening they are sitting in the hotel garden instead of facing the sea.

After a couple of glasses of red wine, Yvonne turns to Huda and asks her if she's enjoyed the day. She doesn't expect her friend to answer, and lets out a deep sigh: 'The sea made me remember, no, not remember, because I hadn't forgotten, the sea brought me face to face with my family and Lebanon and everything again, and made me realise for the first time how these memories ruin my life.'

'Me too, me too!'

'No! You too!'

'OK, OK, let's forget. The best thing is for us to forget, just like the proverb says, "Talk to the sea, it won't tell."'

'But we were so enthusiastic about this holiday! Is it possible that when we arrived we began dancing with joy at the sight of the sea, and now we're avoiding even talking about it, as if it was going to infect us with some awful disease?'

The iPhone breaks in on Huda's melancholy as she is about to go to bed, ringing with messages that obliterate the past and thrust her into the present. Three messages from her secretary in Toronto. Huda's heart lurches as she reads that the biggest potential backer of her play has been in touch asking to see the whole text before he commits to financing it. *I'll have to go back to Toronto tomorrow,* she thinks in a panic, picturing the holiday cancelled.

Huda had contacted a big Arab-Canadian financier in Toronto, telling him that she wanted to direct a stage version of *One Thousand and One Nights*, and how the play was going to tell the Canadians and the West about a whole new side of Arab and Muslim culture. She said she'd read around a thousand pages of the book and decided to find someone to write her an adaptation for the theatre, a play that would be about a time of passion and openness that lay at the heart of these magical-realist stories.

'That's music to my ears,' the man had cried enthusiastically. 'I'm behind this project heart and soul!'

Huda calls her secretary at once. 'What's going on?'

She listens to what the secretary has to say, full of apprehension as she sees herself landing in Toronto and making straight for the backer's office, Najib is his name, talking to him, arguing with him, smiling at him. 'Fine, I'm coming tomorrow,' she shouts at the secretary. She rushes to Yvonne's room, banging on the door, telling her she's leaving.

'OK, I get it, you're going home. But why? Has someone died?'

'Yes. My play's about to die. The backer wants to strangle it.'

'OK, I understand. Thank God he hasn't strangled it yet. Let's think of a solution.'

Breathlessly, Huda tells Yvonne how the Arab actor she'd chosen for the role of Shahrazad met the backer at a party and enthused over her part, adding that the Canadians would be shocked by the play, and would never believe it was an Arab play and all the actors were Arabs. 'What a stupid girl! She probably flashed her eyes at him and stuck her tits out, then he got worried about his reputation and didn't want to have his name associated with the play after all. He should have been proud that it had the potential to change the West's view of us, and show them that we can be bold in our art, not just in acts of destruction.'

Yvonne stands up. 'Come on, Huda. Let's have a glass of wine. I have a great solution.'

'You mean you'll think of a solution after you've had a drink?'

'No, I've already thought of a great solution. OK, let's sit first, then we'll go to the terrace to celebrate.'

Yvonne had a watertight plan: Huda would contact the backer and tell him that at present there was no complete text. 'I'm going to rely on rehearsals, experimentation, discussions with the actors, so we create the text together, but I understand completely if you've changed your mind and want to pull out, as there are plenty of Canadian backers only too happy to step forward. I prefer to have you, of course, as you're Arab-Canadian and your name's well known.'

'At this point *I* come into the picture,' continues Yvonne, 'and try to help by putting you in touch with backers from England.'

Huda jumps to her feet and throws herself on Yvonne. 'You're brilliant.'

'I know!'

Huda hurries to her phone to punch out her email to the backer with some force. 'It's not my pornography you should be scared of,' she mutters to herself.

'Listen,' Yvonne urges her, 'tell him you'll show him the text when it's ready. Of course in reality he won't see a single word of it until it's being performed!'

Huda doesn't close her eyes until the first light of dawn, exactly when Shahrazad sighs and whispers coyly to King Shahrayar, 'My lord', as drowsiness overcomes her. Huda has chosen this play to show that women's wiles are merely a product of their longing to control their own destinies. Now she embraces all of them beneath her closed eyelids.

It's the following evening and the sky is a playground for the swallows, who are like a group of small children darting here and there until their mothers call them in to get ready for bed, while Huda and Yvonne, dressed to kill, hope the night will only end at dawn. They wait for Roberto and Lucio on the hotel terrace. 'You know, Yvonne, yesterday, when I was having nightmares about whether I'd manage to get the play out or not, I promised myself that I would never complain or lose my temper again, and that nothing was important compared to financing my play. But the moment I heard the backer had agreed to finance it after all, I forgot my promise, and now look at the state I'm in. I'm really tense, I'm obsessed by the feeling that Roberto isn't going to show up this evening, even though he promised.'

'Are you making fun of me, Huda? Please don't try to beat me at my own game. I'm the one who's always fearful and apprehensive, not you. One of us is enough! And I have to face the fact that when Lucio promised to pass by the hotel, he was just teasing me. I don't know why promises made at night feel as if they'll never be kept, the opposite of promises made in the daytime.'

'Don't worry, I won't leave you alone in the hotel if Lucio doesn't keep his promise.'

'You too, don't worry.'

'Has it occurred to you that we're behaving like adolescents?'

'I don't understand what you mean.'

'We know very well that nothing's going to come of our relationships with these men. All we really want is someone to while away the time with, make us feel desirable, take an interest in us. And yet we're so anxious that they won't show up. Anyone would think it was a matter of life or death.'

They laugh. 'It's all Lebanon's fault,' comments Huda. 'We left when we were teenagers and we've never grown up.'

Lucio takes them both by surprise. They shriek together delightedly: 'Lucio, Lucio', as if he's a policeman rescuing them from a gang of criminals.

Yvonne goes off with Lucio, seeing and hearing nothing, consumed by the fear that things might not go as she desperately hopes they will. She has to convince herself that he's a one-night stand, no more and no less. She makes a big effort to appear cheerful and carefree and ensure that he doesn't disappear before he's slept with her.

'Shall we go to a restaurant? I'm inviting you!'

Immediately she is embarrassed by the dregs of the past, her way of treating men, trying to buy them with fancy meals and invitations to restaurants, but he deserves to be spoiled today!

She persists. 'Are you hungry?'

He shows her to a restaurant where the sea almost touches her shoes. She smiles broadly at him, encouraging him, as they examine the menu, to order the same as her. He hesitates over whether to order a glass of wine for himself until he hears her ordering a whole bottle; she's been brought up on the saying 'The way to a man's heart is through his stomach', but the wine has another function, to make his head swim.

She notices how he eats and drinks slowly and thoughtfully, the opposite of her family who, whenever she invited them to a restaurant during her visits to Lebanon, would devour everything in front of them, leaving the plates shiny and white like cats and dogs. They would always choose the most famous and expensive restaurants, until she eventually realised that common sayings like 'Generosity generates happiness' and 'Feed someone and they'll be obliged to you' were just big lies.

The wine begins to change little by little into a Botox injection, instant cosmetic surgery, reinforcing her feeling that she is beautiful and desirable, especially because Lucio picks up where he left off on the beach, flirting openly with her, paying no attention to the people around them in the restaurant. When the bill arrives and he reaches for his pocket, attempting to contribute, she hurries to pick up the bill and pay. As soon as they are outside the restaurant he suggests taking her to the highest point in the town so that she can see 'a view like nothing else on earth'. Her heart rejoices. Is it possible that there are still romantic men in this world, dreamers like him?

He takes her along streets and alleyways whose gardens give off a perfume of jasmine and honeysuckle. Every time she sees a beautiful house, she imagines herself living in it with Lucio. *I really am crazy! Huda's quite right. Even a teenager doesn't imagine life with a boy she's going out with for the first time. Tick tock tick tock. That must be the waiting eggs' clock ticking. Tick tock tick tock.* She begins to worry about how to smuggle him into her room that night with everybody watching. When they have been walking for around twenty minutes, she starts to feel uneasy. Maybe he's changed his mind about her. Otherwise how can he wait so patiently to be alone with her somewhere private?

He studies medicine and is trying to apply what he's learnt about digesting food before having sex, she tells herself.

They reach the town's old fort, illuminated like a giant star, and climb steps through the heart of a small wood, redolent with the pungent smell of pine and cinchona trees that settles in her head like a delicious drug.

A big box rests between the branches of a sycamore tree; it stirs Yvonne's imagination and she takes a picture of it to use in one of her advertisements.

'Yvonne, get ready to take an even better picture!'

He purses his lips and begins whistling and a dove emerges from the box and perches in its entrance as if to enquire what's going on.

He whistles again and a second dove emerges, and a third and a fourth, until the outside of the box is crowded with doves on its roof and its sides, cooing and inspecting Lucio and Yvonne, curious to know what these visitors want. Yvonne carries on clicking, taking photos with her phone.

'Who do these dovecotes belong to?'

'Not to me, that's for sure!' and he leans her against the tree and kisses her greedily on her lips and neck and hair. She returns his kisses, trying to slow him down, because she likes taking her time. She likes the kiss to breathe inside her gently until its warmth spreads all through her body. When she doesn't succeed in slowing him down, she thinks about giving in. Let him do what he wants. They have the whole night ahead of them and she can make him go slower once they are alone together in her room. But when his hand reaches under her dress, and with his other hand he begins taking out his prick, just as with his whistling he managed to bring out the first dove from its house, she whispers to him, 'Let's go to my room.'

'*Si, si,*' he answers her, but he is almost inside, and then he is. She tries to keep her balance, afraid her foot will slip, and when she anchors herself firmly to the tree trunk it begins to scrape her back, while Lucio carries on with what he's doing as if he is knocking a nail into her, despite her fidgeting. He stops suddenly, whispering to her: 'Yvonne, hurry up. I've come, I've come.'

She pretends that she's come too, pulling him to her, violently squeezing his lower half as if trying to make sure none of the sperm escapes. But is it possible to get impregnated standing up? She is obsessed with the idea of having a child before it's too late, wanting a relationship with a man just so she can become a mother and create a family. The child would make the two of them blend like labneh and za'atar: neither labneh nor za'atar tastes so delicious on its own. But every man, whether she was in a stable relationship with him or not, was afraid for his sperm, as if it was the only currency he possessed, and pulled out of her even if he'd checked that she'd taken precautions.

She has been pregnant twice, when she was twenty, then again when she was twenty-eight. The first time, the man she was in a relationship with was delighted and asked her to marry him at once, but she was completely immersed in her studies and the father didn't have a well-paid job. The second time she was blissfully happy to find she was pregnant, but the one who had sowed his seed in her, instead of feeling love and tenderness because there was something of him in her womb, immediately began to blame her and accuse her of wanting to trap him, of being jealous of his freedom and wanting to imprison him, urging her to end the thing at once.

She still remembers how he didn't go with her to the doctor, or offer to pay even a part of the costs, how she had been consumed with regret when she opened her eyes and heard the doctor saying, 'We're done here. Everything's fine,' discovering what stood between her and the maternal instinct that had wanted to preserve the foetus.

Lucio has withdrawn at the last minute and come on her thigh. She is about to give him an almighty shove, so he will roll all the way down the hill and into the town, but she sticks to her promise to herself on this holiday to be submissive to men to the end, make herself believe that a woman is a man's shadow, follow, not lead. *I wonder if he's stained my beautiful dress?*

She begins trembling, eyes closed, pretending that her pleasure has made her lose the power of speech. She takes his hand, kissing it and sighing a long sigh, and doesn't let go as they leave the woods. The doves must have been the only witnesses to her disappointment. The climb up the hill was full of expectation. Now she feels as if she's walking downhill alone. When they are back in the noise and bustle, she stops at a bar, saying she wants to go in. He agrees gladly, and they drink a Martini and a Cinzano.

With more Martinis and Cinzanos there are more embraces, whispering, happiness. They cross through the hubbub of the town to her hotel. She summons up her courage and flings herself on him before they go in, so he kisses her at length. *Who says I'm with him now because I want to get pregnant? I feel as if I'm lying in the branches of a tall tree, suspended between the sky and the earth, with no thoughts or responsibilities, happy in the warmth of his arms.*

'What's this historic kiss between Lebanon and Italy?' she says to him, laughing as she walks towards the hotel door, while he remains where he is. 'Don't be afraid. Nobody's going to object.'

He comes up to her and kisses her briefly on the cheek this time.

'I have to join my friends. We're going back to Rome early tomorrow morning.'

He reaches into his shirt pocket and takes out a card: 'This is my email. Let's be in touch! I've really enjoyed getting to know you. I'd like to visit you in London one day.'

'I thought you were staying till Sunday. For three days.'

'No, no, we're going back to Rome. *Ciao*, Yvonne, *ciao*.'

'Let's go into the hotel,' she whispers, unable to believe what she's hearing.

When he kisses her again on both cheeks, she descends on his lips, trying to immobilise him and imprison him, but he disengages himself from her clutches with his usual agility.

'Bye, lovely Yvonne, *ciao*,' and he turns his back on her and vanishes.

'Lucio, *ciao*, you bastard.' She goes into the hotel and asks for her room key then rushes outside, intending to go after him, but stops herself and hurries to the bar and drinks a whisky this time, then another.

'Lucio is like my hotel key: as soon as I hand it in, it becomes somebody else's property,' she says to Huda, when she comes back from her date with Roberto. 'At least I behaved like a woman with him. I didn't kick him or smash his teeth in.'

But it was Lucio who eventually rolled *her* from the top of the mountain to the valley bottom, while she was in the process of recovering from the annoyance that choked her every time she thought of what happened. She forced herself to go back to the same beach the next morning, to the rocks that had witnessed her happiness. When her feelings of dejection got the better of her she asked the sea to console her, so it rocked her and played with her as if she was a child, soothing her fury and resentment. But the sea's efforts turned out to be in vain, as did Huda's attempts to cheer her up. Huda and Roberto took her to a restaurant on the beach, accessible only by boat, and the moment the three of them entered amid the noise of people and raucous music and dancers spraying champagne on each other, her gaze alighted on Lucio in the embrace of a young woman. Their arms and legs were intertwined and they were making love with their eyes.

'It's Lucio,' muttered Yvonne, frozen to the spot, in spite of the fact that everything had begun to spin around her at a dreadful speed. 'Look, everybody, look at the whore. He said he was leaving town.'

She didn't come to her senses until she was outside the restaurant, leaning on Huda and Roberto, her mouth dry. 'I hope God dries his spit so he explodes and dies. He had his fill of me and pissed on me like a dog, then he ran away.'

'You're still angry?' asks Huda later that evening. 'But don't forget that the two of you meeting was like when a train stops in the station for a few moments then leaves again.'

'And Roberto? Wasn't he like a train stopping at your station, and yet he's still here? He even hired a little boat just for you so he could take you to that beach. Lucio must have really despised me. I thought my pride was like a turtle's shell that nobody could dent, and it turns out it's like a soap bubble. I don't understand! Why do they make love with me once or twice then rush away as if I have a barrelful of acid between my legs?'

63

'Listen, Yvonne, remember what Eve said to Adam when he asked her why she fell in love with him. "There was nobody else, you shit!"'

Yvonne smiles, then collapses into laughter and embraces Huda, but almost at once she begins weeping bitterly. 'I was ovulating and I thought I could get pregnant from a handsome Italian boy, charming, a medical student, with no morals, as it turns out. Great characteristics for the offspring!'

'Yvonne, surely you don't want to be pregnant without letting the father know?'

'Why not? Instead of throwing his sperm into the garbage, he can throw it into my womb in blissful ignorance. Isn't that better for everyone?'

Everyone has a baby, Yvonne thinks, *my sister, mother, aunts, grandmother, great-great-great grandmothers, even women who are forced to have sex, have babies. For heaven's sake, even a female courgette flower makes its own baby courgettes and when it doesn't work, if the insects are blind or have blocked noses, it can be fertilised by a human hand.*

Huda feels sad and as if she's letting Yvonne down, because her wonderful night with Roberto is still going on in her mind. After they'd left her hotel and walked through the narrow alleyways, he'd taken her hand and said: 'Huda, let me show you something extraordinary.'

He hurries her along as if the thing he wants her to see is going to disappear in a few moments. He takes her down uninhabited streets, which seems odd to her. Why don't people realise that you only get to know a place properly when you see where the locals live?

'Sorry, you must be hungry. But I really want to show you something I think will fascinate you.'

He rings a bell and a guard opens the large gate for them. He greets Roberto warmly. Huda finds herself in a forest of pine trees, their tops lit up as if their hair has suddenly gone white. In the midst of them is an illuminated glass building, shaped like a pyramid. Roberto leads her towards it, and when he pushes open the door and a strong smell of damp is released, Huda recoils in horror, afraid for her hair, and invents an excuse.

'I can't go in, sorry, I have asthma and the damp is bad for me.' She puts a hand to her hair, feeling it, convinced that it's already started to go frizzy.

'Oh sorry, sorry, I'll go in then and show you from a distance.'

She sees Roberto standing in front of a 'European' date tree, as they were known in Lebanon, because they were barren and unable to produce dates; princess's fans, children called them. Roberto points to its luxuriant branches with their white flowers, looking upwards and indicating the highest point on the tree, then lowering his hand to pick up the broken fan-shaped branches on the ground.

'It's the suicidal palm tree,' he explains to her enthusiastically as he emerges.

'Suicidal tree?'

'Yes, it died by its own hand. Perhaps I'll bring you tomorrow so that you can see it in daylight.'

'But I saw it very clearly, just as if I was inside,' she replies quickly, scared that he will bring her here tomorrow, her and Yvonne, and Yvonne will go inside with him while she remains outside, touching her hair, fearful of the damp.

No, don't be jealous of Yvonne, Huda tells herself, looking at Roberto. 'I just don't want to bother you again.' She remembers how Yvonne dragged Roberto against his will to go swimming in the sea with her, the day they met him, and how he resisted her as she jumped on him, diving underwater, teasing him, trying to race him. When

Yvonne came back to the beach Huda had said to her in Arabic, 'We understand, Madam Yvonne, that you're an excellent swimmer, but don't forget: fish are good at swimming too.'

'Roberto, can you tell me what you meant when you said that this palm tree kills itself?'

'Once this tree starts flowering it never stops, it keeps flowering and flowering until it collapses and dies. It's from Madagascar. The owner of the villa asked me to plant strange trees for him. He liked its name, "the blessed one", and he was lucky because it flowered seven years after it was planted – he was afraid that he would die before it flowered, because it often takes decades. But tell me, Huda, does this asthma stop you swimming or doing sport in general?'

'No, not at all. It just bothers me in saunas or glass buildings, or maybe in the Amazon if we go there this evening.'

'Fine, fine, shall we go to the villa? I've prepared some food.'

They enter the villa where he lives while he's working in the gardens. The curtains have long embraced the sun and their pinkness has faded; ivory-coloured sheets cover the furniture, and the sleeping mirror has draped itself in a light veil like smoke.

Does Roberto choose to live in this dim light, or maybe the lamps only want to see the family who originally lived in the villa? They are no longer here, but their faces remain, calm and familiar, looking down from the paintings hanging on the walls with faint smiles on their lips, as if they are waiting to see what the landscape architect and this woman are going to do now they are alone together.

I wonder if he brings a lot of women here, thinks Huda to herself. It's as if the whole atmosphere, from the suicidal palm tree to the dim light inside, has reminded her of the beautiful, seductive woman in *One Thousand and One Nights*, who used to kill her lovers if sleep overcame them while they waited for her in her garden, or if they reached out their hands to her laden table before she appeared.

'Is this table normally your desk?' she asks him, trying to overcome the awkwardness that has begun to accumulate between them.

Roberto has set the table in a corner of the vast room and lit candles that make shadows on the roses. She gasps at the beauty of the tablecloth and begins touching the embroidery on it.

'There's a story to this tablecloth,' says Roberto. 'A young woman from this town embroidered it and she kept postponing her marriage until she reached the final stitch, and then it was too late for her to marry. Can you imagine? She was twenty.'

'Twenty years old and she was on the shelf?' interrupts Huda. 'Or perhaps she was like me and was against the idea of marriage!'

'Really?'

She has discovered over time that whenever she admitted this, it aroused men, maybe because they didn't believe in marriage either, and liked the idea that they could attract her without any promise of a commitment, or maybe because they liked the idea of trying to change her mind.

'The lady of the house here, the wife of the duke, sent for the young woman, wanting to buy the tablecloth from her as it had become famous. When she spread it out on the table, and her husband saw the tears and ears of corn and crosses embroidered on it in the most beautiful stitching, he began contemplating the eyes and fingers of the pretty seamstress, who had become an old maid without noticing and continued to live in the world she had designed on the table cover. The husband fell passionately in love with her and declared his love, but the seamstress rejected all his advances, despite the allure of money and status. When he insisted that she tell him why she had rejected him and she said that he was almost her father's age, he took his revenge by removing the cover from the table and throwing it under his shoes in the bottom of his wardrobe. The wife thought her husband had gone mad, as everything about him had changed overnight.

'When death overtook him and the widow's eyes fell on the abandoned cover, she was once again struck by its beauty and asked the seamstress to add an angel on each of its four edges in memory of the duke. She agreed immediately, delighted at the return of the cover from under the shoes to the tabletop, so that it could see the light of day again. She finished embroidering the four angels in the corners of the cloth, but nobody contemplating its beauty could guess what each angel held in his hand: Was it an apple or a beetle or maybe the sun? And the seamstress did not divulge the secret of what the angels were holding in their hands until after the widow had gone to join her husband.'

Huda brings her face up close to the cloth and sees the hearts and rosebuds and little birds and ears of corn and the four angels and puts her fingers on something resembling a pear. 'Are these pears?'

Roberto laughs and says somewhat hesitantly: 'The seamstress had her revenge on the man who hid the cloth under his shoes, by making the angels squeeze a man's testicles.'

After they have finished eating and drunk the wine, Huda stands up to help him collect the plates, then goes to the bathroom to brush her teeth as she always does when she thinks she is about to have sex with someone. She rushes out to him and, just as she imagined herself doing when they kissed the day she met him, she undoes his shirt buttons and his belt, leaving him to undo the rest as she notices the astonishment on his face, then she brings her lips down to his neck, his hairless chest, his waist, his stomach. She pauses briefly, then carries on below his stomach and when she reaches his thighs, he moves restlessly and takes hold of her hand. He leads her into his room where the humidity and heat of the day mix with the cold of the night, the walls are peeling and the patterns have faded. A big mosquito net hangs down over the sofa bed.

She takes off her own clothes and pulls him to her, seeing his surprise, and his excitement and desire for her escalating. She knows what's going on in his head. *Is this the same woman I saw holding on to the iron railing, staring at the sea in such sorrow and confusion that I was afraid she was going to jump in?*

She kicks the clothes away with her bare foot and holds Roberto tight and clings to him. Instead of laying her down, he begins kissing her neck and her back: 'How I've longed to be alone with you since we were on the beach. I didn't think there was any hope of it.'

They fall on each other, their bodies intertwining like a man and a woman in a Picasso painting. He disentangles himself and kisses her again. She doesn't want to wait. She takes hold of his hand and pulls him down on to the bed and finds herself on top of him. She begins to flower like the suicidal palm tree, nectar pouring from her until they collapse together, then he tries to lift her off him, but she pulls him to her, murmuring 'Don't worry, don't worry,' thinking to herself, *I don't care if he makes me pregnant. I can always get an abortion.*

'You're a witch! I have to admit you made me feel as if I was the female, wanting to take, instead of worrying about how to satisfy you.'

'Thanks very much for the compliment – I think!'

'Sorry, Huda, if I repeat the question: Are you the Muslim or Yvonne?'

'I'm the Muslim and she's the Christian!'

'I've been confused this evening. You're as liberated as any Western woman, if not more so. I won't hide it from you, I was shocked, I wasn't expecting … So you're a Muslim! You're great at sex!'

Huda was not especially surprised to hear this. *Maybe it's* because *I'm a Muslim,* she thought, and her mind went back to her childhood.

Huda was no more than seven years old when she went with her mother to visit a relative and Sawsan, this woman's daughter, took her out to play with the girls who lived nearby. One of the games they played was new to her. It was called 'the bee and the wasp' and when Huda's turn came, she had to stand back to back with Sawsan, they linked arms, then she lifted Huda off the ground. Sawsan told Huda to call out, 'I'm the bee', then lowered her so that she could lift Sawsan up on her back and she could shout, 'I'm the wasp', and so on.

Huda loved this game, especially when she was the one being lifted, her face to the sky; and also because she discovered she was strongly built and could raise Sawsan high in the air. When Huda went home and there weren't any girls in her neighbourhood to play with, she wished she could teach her brother the new game, even though he was six years older, but she knew in her heart of hearts that it was impossible. She didn't remember playing with her brother at all – she wasn't even allowed to enter his room. Huda waited until the next day to tell her school friends about the bee and the wasp, and in no time the school playground had turned into dozens of games of bees and wasps. Up and down, up and down they went, on each other's backs, calling in turn, 'I'm the bee', 'I'm the wasp'. One day Huda's mother happened to come into her bedroom and see Huda and a friend back to back, with Huda high up in the air, legs waving around as she laughed and shouted, 'I'm the wasp'. Her mother attacked the girls like a mad bull. Their intertwined arms separated and they collapsed on to the hard tiled floor. They were terrified of her furious, disgusted eyes, as she lashed out at them: 'For shame! I never imagined my daughter would sink so low!' Then she slapped Huda round the face.

'What have we done?' Huda asked, crying. 'We were just playing the bee and the wasp, the game that Sawsan taught us.'

This seemed to rekindle her fury, for she rushed to the kitchen and returned clutching a red chilli pepper. She began rubbing it on Huda's lips and tongue, holding her head tightly with her other hand to keep her still. You'd think she'd never tasted one of those peppers in her life, and she clearly felt no pity for Huda as her face turned to fire and the choking sensation in her throat almost stopped her from breathing. She finished by shouting in a frenzy, 'Every time you think of the bee and the wasp, I want you to remember the red chilli pepper!'

But hadn't Huda heard her mother describe hard-working people as being like bees? And wasn't a wasp just an ugly-looking bee? At school Huda had learnt that bees were intelligent and knew when it was going to rain and were superior to human architects, building houses out of wax in exactly equal hexagonal shapes without any tools. Bees were famous for being clean, for they constructed coffins out of wax when one of them died, so that the beehive didn't smell, then got rid of the coffin as soon as possible. And every time she or her brothers had a stomach ache, their mother gave them a spoonful of honey, while her grandmother mixed honey with musk to put around her eyes to stop them watering.

The burning of the chilli on her lips stayed for a long time and she felt it every time she was with a man. As the unmarried daughter of their neighbours was daring enough to explain, the game of the bee and the wasp was like a re-enactment of cats coupling in February, when male and female cats clung together, miaowing loudly, and annoying the grown-ups who poured water over them and shouted at them and tried to distract them from their embraces with pieces of meat, all to no avail.

She always tries to be content to remember only the burning in her mouth, because even the chilli pepper itself doesn't want to remember the time it rubbed her backside. Chillis grow and flourish so that they can be added to food in small doses, not to the bottoms of eleven-year-old girls! Her screams reached God and the angels and the dead whose souls had gone to heaven, but apparently not her mother as she continued rubbing the pepper on her bottom. As she screamed, Huda was convinced her mother had finally gone mad, and was so confused that she thought the hole where her food came out was actually her mouth.

They were three girls and one boy – Issam, the dyer's son. His father used to hang the clothes and fabrics that he'd washed and dyed in the garden next to his shop. They slipped in through the back gate at a signal from Issam, to play with the dyes, but then started playing doctors and patients. They all took off their underpants and one by one, the girls lifted up their dresses in front of 'Doctor'

Issam, who merely looked, then gasped in horror and announced that the cases was extremely grave and the only cure in such difficult cases was for them to look at the doctor's 'pigeon'. His pigeon didn't look anything like a pigeon, more like a thick lily that hadn't yet flowered.

Suddenly they heard the laughter of their neighbour Farouk, who had caught them when he came into the garden through the shop, looking for the tops of Coca-Cola bottles to replace lost backgammon pieces. His laughter and kindly words – 'Go on, kids, why don't you go back to your own homes now?' – deluded them into believing they were just children playing children's games, but when they scattered like ants on a sugar lump blown away by a sudden puff of wind, the game turned deadly serious and the punishment was terrible. First Fatima, who was tied to the door handle for a whole day, without food or drink and without being allowed to go to the toilet so she wet herself and was beaten for not holding her pee in. Then Nadira, whose mother tried to rub chilli on her bottom at the suggestion of her grand-mother; but when Nadira passed out, her mother had to make do with rubbing chilli on her mouth, so she came round coughing and wailing. Nadira's mother's failure to get the chilli where she had originally wanted it must have been the spur for Huda's mother to succeed, since she was the shaykh's daughter, who had to be a model of good behaviour, an example to all. Later Huda used to think about Issam, son of the dye-shop owner, who had never been punished, while she screamed in pain at the burning sensations that spread up into her eyes and then settled in her nose. Issam made them do it; wasn't it his fault? Yet Huda saw him a few days later laughing loudly and pointing at his bottom, as he told his mates about the monkey that sat on the chilli pepper and jumped up and down in the air. The story of Huda's burning bottom went all around the neighbourhood and everybody was talking about it. *I'll get my revenge on all of you, you'll see,* she shouted to herself.

But this threat of Huda's was redirected at herself a few years later when her father died suddenly of a heart attack. She was sure God intervened in the lives of His servants, especially if they were believers. God had taken pity on her father when he saw his daughter half-naked in a swimsuit, not wanting him to remember the sight whenever he looked at her, so He instantly released him from his suffering.

That day she began covering her hair from genuine conviction. All that showed were her hands. Her dress reached well below her knees. She no longer felt weighed down like before and tried to be passive, like her mother and most of the girls in the family, going from home to school and back again, letting life move sluggishly along on crutches, and being as her parents wished her to be: neither female nor male, not even human. She began blocking her ears to songs, whispered promises of love and all worldly enticements, in case God poured molten tin and metal in her ears and repeatedly flayed the skin off her body in the fires of hell. The man who taught them about religion had described this fire: 'God spent a thousand years gathering wood for it, and a thousand years burning the wood until the fire grew red, and a thousand more years until it was black.'

'Is this your first time since breaking up with him?' Roberto is asking her now, hesitantly, his voice like cool water extinguishing the flames, and so she frees Fatima's hand from the doorknob, puts ice on Nadira's lips, and feels loving and affectionate.

'Yes. And you, what's your situation?'

'I'm in a long-term relationship. She's in India now, teaching Italian in New Delhi.'

'India! She's very far away from you.'

'How glad I am that she's far away, especially at this particular moment. Shall I see you tomorrow, Huda?'

'Of course. You don't have to ask.'

'How wonderful you are!'

He holds her close.

'Will you take me to the sea for a few moments?'

'Now?'

'Yes, please.'

He takes her to the sea that lies under a beautiful dark blanket and she can hear it whispering to her joyfully: *'Your father's death is not your fault.' 'But why did he die the day he saw me in a swimsuit?' 'Chance. Sheer chance. Your father suffered from heart disease. Everyone knew that. The Creator created me so that people could embrace me, gaze at me, feel at peace with themselves and enjoy my fruits.'*

'Thanks, Roberto.'

He holds her close again and kisses her tenderly.

Because every journey has a beginning and an end, the two friends left the Italian Riviera four days later to go back to Rome. Yvonne cried constantly, even when she was sitting on the toilet, and looked everywhere for Lucio so that she could punch him. But the moment she set foot in Rome, her sadness began to diminish and as the beauty of the ancient city gently encompassed her, the horrible taste in her mouth gradually went away. The tall columns, the sculptures, the incense in the churches, the eyes of the saints, all of these made her mock her own pride, which had raged at first, then complained and howled like a dog that had been kicked in the stomach. Meanwhile, Huda's attachment to Roberto increased whenever she heard his voice in furtive phone calls, kept secret from Yvonne, in fact every time she heard a man talking away unintelligibly in Italian.

But as soon as Huda began rehearsals for her play, the day after she arrived back in Toronto, the effects of her holiday evaporated. She slept badly, overwhelmed by the play and its huge cast of actors and musicians. Only in the theatre could she sleep soundly, so she would always take a short nap around midday. Meanwhile Yvonne immersed herself, not in the waters of the local pool as she'd promised herself when in Italy, but in sessions with the psychoanalyst, and in getting to know other single women as they tried together to overcome the pain caused by loneliness and childlessness, by accepting it and enjoying it.

PART TWO

The Occasional Virgin

Three months after they met in Italy, Huda and Yvonne go walking in Hyde Park. Huda has come to London for five days to negotiate a deal with a British theatre to show her play *One Thousand and One Nights* after its success in Toronto.

'I'm longing to discover London with you. I still don't know it as I should, even though I've lived here for nearly twenty years,' says Yvonne.

They walk along, noticing all the seasons in the same place at the same time: spring, summer, autumn and winter; from fragrant green grass to brown earth and tall yellow plants whose liveliness has been drained away by the sun; trees bare of leaves and others whose new young leaves have just opened; trees that have preserved their white blossoms, under the illusion that it is still spring. Black crows fly down from the trees and land on the ground, while the pigeons crowd together, one of them dropping some food.

'I've never seen such big crows in my life. They look like birds of prey, eagles even!'

'Don't look at them, Huda. They're bad luck.'

'I've always liked crows and owls. I felt sorry for them when I was little because people hated them so much. I remember I used to defend them and remind people that they were God's creatures just like us.'

'Of course. You always have to be different.'

'I like their personalities, how owls prefer to live in desolate places, and ruins and old empty caves and the tops of church towers. And did you know that crows can pick out the best kinds of dates? So people wait to see which date palm they choose and follow them.'

'So, from now on I'll like owls and crows.'

'Disgusting!' shouts Huda suddenly. 'Kleenex, hurry, Yvonne, before I throw up.'

Yvonne searches through her pockets for a tissue, guessing that a bird has defecated on her friend's face. Not finding one, she bends down and picks up a large leaf and gives it to Huda, who throws it away in revulsion as soon as she brings it near her mouth, and quickly wipes her lips on the sleeve of her jacket.

'Do you think there's some kind of public toilet nearby? Let's buy a bottle of water. Please, I want to wash my mouth.'

They run towards a kiosk that looks from a distance as if there is a demonstration taking place around it. Yvonne arrives ahead of Huda. She buys a bottle of water, after making her way through the groups of people gathered near Speakers' Corner. Huda rubs her lips violently as if trying to clean a tarnished silver jug, then empties the remaining water on the sleeve of her jacket.

'The crow wanted to reward you for your affection, to give you the good news that a guy's going to kiss you on the lips today because you're the choicest of dates.'

'Definitely. The guy who's going to kiss me wants to taste shit. I'm going to throw up.'

They find themselves at the heart of Speakers' Corner, despite the fact that the only thing on Yvonne's mind is a late breakfast – brunch with coffee, the aroma of which would penetrate her brain cells, and eggs fried in olive oil and sumac.

'Come on, Huda, I'm going to die of hunger.'

'I swear I didn't know that women could talk at Speakers' Corner too!'

A woman in her early fifties stands on the lower of two white-painted wooden steps and rests her hands on the upper step. She looks as if she's riding a scooter as she addresses the crowd: 'God created people in vast numbers of races, in order that each race should stay where they are and not stray from their roots. If they emigrate to another country, they disobey the Creator and rebel against His just will.'

'Not true!' shouts Yvonne. 'The Creator has not only blessed the emigration of me and my friend here,' raising Huda's arm high, 'but has given us any amount of help in our new homelands.'

All eyes zoom in on Yvonne and Huda for a few moments before a voice is raised in the crowd. A young Arab man, smartly dressed, sporting a trendy flat-top hairstyle and a dark red leather jacket, calls back to the first speaker: 'Do I understand, my dear Myrtle, that you want your Queen to pack her bags and leave, given that her ancestors were originally German?'

'The Creator's just will? Haven't we already violated the Creator's just will, not only while we were present in the countries we colonised, but after we left too? Have you heard the one about the English officer who used to take out his blue glass eye and put it on his desk, and say to the Sudanese officials whenever he was about to go back to England on annual leave: "Don't think I can't see you when I'm away! This eye of mine will be observing your every move."'

Most of the bystanders applaud this intervention from an elderly Englishman leaning on a walking stick.

'Bravo! You're a good man. I like you!' shouts the Arab in the leather jacket. 'But let me assure Myrtle that there are some English who want us here, in fact they really need us. It's a matter of life and death for them.' He pauses for a moment, then says, 'I'm talking about the beautiful pigs. We're the only ones who like them and treat them with affection and respect. We're kind to them and don't slaughter them and eat them. In fact we want them to remain and procreate.'

The place erupts in laughter and the woman orator shouts: 'You should be shedding tears instead of laughing. You're kind to animals? Is that why you slaughter sheep and cows with knives, with no warning and no sedation so that their meat is halal? Is that what you call kind? It's the height of cruelty.'

'No, no, that's wrong. You're mistaken, my dear Myrtle. The word "halal" doesn't refer to the way the animals or birds are slaughtered, but to the prayer before they're killed.'

A man who looks Turkish comments: 'Halal means that the animal faces Mecca while it's being slaughtered.'

'Mecca?' shouts the young Arab. 'How are we supposed to know the direction of Mecca when it's foggy and rainy all the time?'

An Englishwoman who looks like Vanessa Redgrave calls out: 'And what about us? Don't we throw crabs and lobsters alive into boiling water? Isn't that the height of cruelty?'

'Thank you,' comments the young Arab. 'On behalf of every Muslim in the world I thank you!'

Then the Turkish man intervenes: 'Animals are God's creatures. They have souls just like people. People borrow animals from God Almighty. When they pray for animals' souls it's like them asking God's permission to shed the animals' blood.'

The two women are immediately disillusioned. 'Go, go. Crows really are bad omens.' Huda drags Yvonne away. 'But I'd like to go over to that Arab guy in the leather jacket and say, "I'm a talking animal. Please borrow me from God!"' she says regretfully.

'Halal, halal, oh God!' grumbles Myrtle loudly. 'Will we never be done with this halal?'

'Shhh, Myrtle, don't ask for God's help,' shouts the witty Arab youth, 'or he might come to save you, and then what will you do, when he descends from the sky and settles in Britain and the number of people arriving here goes up by thousands, because of course he'll be surrounded by angels and devils, and they'll take jobs away from the British.'

The laughter of the bystanders suddenly changes to gasps of disapproval as a young man approaches, looking as if he has come straight from the desert – tall and dark-skinned with large, dark, flashing eyes that appear to have kohl round them – and catches hold of the Arab youth's hand, trying to pull him away and repeating, 'Shame on you, shame on you, Tahir.'

Although they are dazzled by his striking physique, both Yvonne and Huda notice his turquoise ring and the silver bracelets round his wrist, which seem out of keeping with his violent behaviour.

'How very rude! He looks North African to me. He's scary!'

'Wow! Have you seen that body? And those eyes! Scary? He can scare me any time. I'd like to tremble in his arms.'

'He looks like someone you couldn't joke with.'

'But you have to agree he's got a nice body.'

Their attention is suddenly caught by a group of laughing people, waving their hands around like birds, then jumping high in the air with their eyes closed, while their leader shouts, 'Laugh louder, louder. Laughter is the new cure for all illnesses. It doesn't discriminate or proscribe. Drink and eat half what you normally do, and laugh four times as much.'

As they leave them behind, they see Tahir, the Arab youth with the dark red jacket, in a circle that has formed around an African monk, there to preach the Gospel and argue against the Quran. 'You British, your forefathers guided us to Christianity, and now you've forgotten what you taught us.'

Huda and Yvonne are about to continue on their way, losing interest in what's going on around them, when something the monk says makes them stop, something to the effect that Islam gets through to the British by way of the food they eat and the shishas they smoke.

'Whenever you inhale the smoke of a shisha, the plague of the shisha gets into your bloodstream. Smoking shishas will lead you astray and make you indolent. As you smoke a shisha, it will whisper to you, "I'm from the land of Islam, Islam, Islam" and brainwash you.'

Amid the eruptions of noisy laughter, Tahir remarks: 'He's right, absolutely right. When I was smoking a shisha yesterday, a jinn came up out of the smoke and bellowed menacingly at me, "You must become a devout, pious and fanatical Muslim at once, or you're a dead man, you're a dead man, you're a dead man." He said it three times, and I began to tremble, as I had no idea how to become a devout, pious and fanatical Muslim. But my wife was cleverer than I was and stripped off in front of the jinn, so he went after her and left me in peace.'

Gales of laughter again, especially from Yvonne: 'We were too quick to leave. He's cute, and smart. He kills me.'

The young Arab salutes the circle with an air kiss, then brings a finger up to his mouth as if requesting their attention.

'Can I ask you a personal question, and I hope you'll be frank with me?'

'Go ahead. What's your question?' says the monk seriously.

'Are you a Muslim?'

'How did you know?' jokes the monk.

Yvonne hurries over to introduce herself to the young Arab man, thinking to herself that Arab men don't bother withdrawing before they come, relying on the woman to take precautions. He merely nods at her before looking up at the sky. Yvonne doesn't understand this behaviour, but raises her head skywards herself, and all in the group copy her. There is nothing to be seen except clouds like white sheep grazing.

'I'm looking for your name in the records of Muslims and I can't find it,' declaims Tahir.

Everyone dissolves into laughter, and the monk replies, 'Of course you won't find it because the Virgin Mary spreads her washing to dry on top of the Muslim names. Did you notice how clean it was?'

Tahir disappears into the crowd. Yvonne comes back, taking hold of Huda's hand and hurrying her in the opposite direction.

'I'm no longer attractive, Huda, I'm sure of it.'

'What happened?'

'I introduced myself to him, but he ignored me completely.'

'He's too busy playing the fool. It would have been better to talk to him after he'd finished his conversation with the monk. Anyway, I noticed he was looking at you as if he really liked you.'

'Thank you for trying to raise my morale.'

'Raise your morale? You're a sex bomb!'

'You mean a time bomb that makes men turn and run the moment they see it.'

'Maybe he ran away because he was shy.'

'Maybe. Come on, let's go and find him.'

They move from one group to another looking for Tahir and discovering that Speakers' Corner is like a popular market, each speaker a vendor calling his wares, as the audience move between groups, until a certain topic or the sound of laughter or a heated dispute attracts them.

'You know, Huda, it's never occurred to me all these years I've been in London to stop and see what's happening at Speakers' Corner. It's really entertaining.'

'And we learn to listen to the opinions of others, even if they're unreasonable or superficial!'

Tahir isn't in the group surrounding the man who looks Jamaican and keeps repeating 'Englishness is whiteness'. This man is rhythmically stamping his feet, so much so that the thumping drowns out his voice. He is holding a couple of posters categorising human beings according to their skin colour – white, Asian, black. He is wearing a military uniform and Nazi-style headgear and his Hitler moustache is out of keeping with the warmth of his eyes and his beautiful white teeth. He pounds the earth with his boots, as if he wants to make a hole in it, and points to the posters: 'This is how the British police see you.'

And he isn't in the group surrounding the young Irishman who is blaming environmental pollution on women's vanity, because their hair dye finds its way into rivers and seas. But they do find him in the biggest group, where a Muslim preacher from Bangladesh is arguing with a black man from South Sudan. It is clear to the two women that the preacher is trying to cover up some slip of the tongue when he says to the black man that there is no future and no honourable life for black people unless they all become Muslims, like Malcolm X and the boxer Muhammad Ali.

The black man is insisting that the preacher show him the Quranic verse that talks about God's love and concern for blacks, while the preacher pretends to look for it in the Quran he has in his hand. At this point, Tahir starts cracking jokes in Arabic: 'A Sudanese whose wife gave birth to a white son told her to put him back in the oven.' Laughter from all those who understand Arabic. 'Have you heard the one about the Sudanese woman who took part in the Miss World beauty competition and won the title of Miss World, the Negative?'

'Shame on you, man,' says a woman wearing a head-scarf. 'How can you be so racist?'

The Bangladeshi preacher closes the Quran, kisses it, then brings it up to his forehead, claiming that he doesn't want to bore his listeners and would rather finish his sermon.

'Why don't you just apologise for lying to me? That would be much better than pretending you can't find it, my brother.'

The preacher's embarrassment, and his worn clothes, make Huda feel sad. Her father used to kiss the Quran, then bring it up to his forehead, and she finds herself intervening. The astonishment that shows on Yvonne's face when she hears her friend speak is nothing to the surprise that Huda herself feels. 'The Quran doesn't mention blacks, but—'

The youth from the desert interrupts her: 'The *Holy* Quran' – emphasising the word 'holy' – 'you have to say the Holy Quran. The two words are inseparable.'

Ignoring him, she goes on, 'But the Prophet Muhammad is the one who said—'

He interrupts her again: 'You have to say "peace be upon him" when you mention the Prophet's name.'

'The Prophet Muhammad is the one who said that an Arab is no better than a non-Arab, unless he is more pious.'

He stands squarely in front of her as if to block off her air supply. 'Are you deaf? You're not talking about your relatives, or a film or a novel. You must add the word "holy" when you mention the Holy Quran, and say "peace be upon him" when the Prophet's name comes up, peace be upon him and his family.'

'God's messenger is the one who ordered the emancipation of slaves and made them free and forbade racism.'

'Substituting the word "messenger" doesn't mean that you don't have to say peace be upon him whenever the name of our Prophet – peace be upon him and his family and companions – comes up. Do you understand?'

'Now leave the sister in peace,' remarks Tahir, 'or do you think you're Jeremy Paxman?'

Warm applause and loud laughter, especially from the British in the audience.

Then the man from the desert addresses himself to Huda. 'If a person is going to talk about religion, he should clean his mouth out before he utters a single syllable, or else keep it shut.'

When Huda merely stares at him without answering, Yvonne says angrily, 'Should I reply to him since you're keeping quiet?'

'No,' remarks Huda in a voice loud enough for him to hear. 'With some people silence can be more powerful and eloquent than words.'

The man from the desert shifts his gaze from Yvonne back to Huda, then shakes his head as if he can't be bothered with them and goes on his way. As soon as he has gone, Yvonne says, 'Journey of No Return!' And they laugh because it's the title of a popular song about a guy in prison who's never coming out.

'I'm going to die of hunger. What do you think about eating here?'

'Let's do it.'

They move away from the groups of people and the noisy voices, taking the paved footpath around Hyde Park until they reach the opposite side of the lake where swans, seagulls, ducks and pigeons jostle together, competing over the bread and crisps and popcorn that people walking in the park have thrown down for them.

As soon as they find a table in the Lido Café, Huda slumps into a chair and sighs deeply. 'I know he's hateful,' says Yvonne, 'that's why I wanted you to shout back at him. He thinks he's got the monopoly on religion. How dare he talk to you as if he was swatting flies! If I were a Muslim, I'd have given him a bloody nose.'

'Do you have to be a Muslim to teach him a lesson?'

'So that I don't seem like a fanatic, or a sectarian.'

Huda laughs: 'I've just thought of a suitable name for him, Ta'abbata Sharran! Ta'abbata Sharran means "the one who held evil under his arm". It's the nickname of a pre-Islamic poet. His mother saw him going out with his sword under his arm, and when someone asked where he was, she said, "He put evil under his arm and went out."'

'Ta'abbata Sharran. It suits him. It's a great name! If you'd thought of it before, I would have called him that to his face.'

'Then he would have beaten us up for comparing him to a pre-Islamic poet!'

They both choose a tomato and mushroom omelette. Yvonne stops eating when there is still more than half of her dish left.

'I'm full.'

'How can you be full?'

'And because I won't be going to the gym today. Don't forget I've got a wedding reception to go to later, and my dress is tight round the waist.'

'But we walked from your house for about an hour, and if you like we can go back on foot.'

'Great, and I'll leave you in the flat while I'm at the hairdresser's, unless you've changed your mind and you'll come with me to the wedding. Please say you will. Please!'

'That would be difficult, since I don't know either the bride or the groom.'

'You know what, thank God I didn't eat like a pig. My dress will fit me now.'

'You're mean, you let me eat my food and your leftovers!'

They begin walking among the children and their families who are flying colourful paper kites, shaped like birds of prey.

'You know, Huda, the analyst who helped me a lot this year assured me that going for walks in parks and gardens did me as much good as talking to her. She said observing the constant transformation in nature – the leaves changing colour, the buds, the flowers, the green returning to cover the bare branches – would give me hope that my life too would change just as nature does, and things wouldn't always remain the same for me.'

'Certainly. She's absolutely right,' answers Huda. Initially when she decided to visit the theatre in London she hadn't wanted to hear about her friend's emotional problems, but when they met face to face she was glad to see her and felt ashamed for being so selfish.

Huda had grown increasingly annoyed in Toronto, when she was obliged to listen to Yvonne for hours, sometimes even in the middle of the night, in phone calls and messages about this man or that, and about her perennial bad luck, the doctor who urged her to have a child before it was too late, all this as she shouted, laughed, cried and cursed, because she wasn't in a relationship, and because she was scared she would never have a child. Huda felt suffocated the moment Yvonne began relating to her what she had said to this or that man and what he had said to her, what she was wearing at the time and how her hair was done.

Huda had even stopped telling Yvonne about her own relationships in case it made her envious, more resentful of her situation, but she found it hard not to tell her how she had had to extricate herself from the arms of Mark, the actor who had taken her to the airport. The day she had begun rehearsals of *One Thousand and One Nights* in Toronto, as she shook one of the new cast members by the hand, she found herself reaching up involuntarily to a small book sticking out of his shirt pocket and discovering that it was Pirandello's *The Man with the Flower in His Mouth*. 'Do you know it?' he'd asked her in undisguised amazement, when she asked him what he thought of it. Hardly a week had gone by before she and Mark were in each other's arms, the mutual attraction too strong to resist.

They pass by Speakers' Corner again on their way out of Hyde Park. This is deliberate on Yvonne's part as she has hopes of running into Tahir and talking to him.

A man in his seventies is standing leaning against the iron railings, holding leaflets that he offers silently to everyone who passes him. People go on their way with a sympathetic shake of their heads. It seems he is asking the British government to help Iraq look for the antiquities that have been looted from the Baghdad Museum. Huda and Yvonne talk to him and learn that he used to be in charge of a section of the museum.

Meanwhile an Indian-looking youth approaches the man, offering him a cup of tea and a biscuit. The man takes the cup hesitantly, while the youth goes back to stand behind a table laden with publications, dominated by a photo of what looks like an Indian maharajah. As Huda and Yvonne pass by, the youth hurries to give them a booklet about the Ahmadiyya doctrine, reciting quietly, 'Can I introduce you to Mirza Ghulam Ahmad, a saviour like the Lord Jesus Christ, the Mahdi, the eleventh imam,' but another hand reaches for it before them and takes it and throws it back on the table.

The hand belongs to Ta'abbata Sharran. He shouts at the Indian youth, who barely comes up to his chest: 'Superstitious nonsense and heresy! An impostor who claimed that he came to this world to guide it.'

'Leave him alone,' Yvonne rebukes him.

'Don't interfere in things that don't concern you.'

'Don't *you* interfere in what doesn't concern *you*. Are you stalking us, by the way?'

Huda takes the booklet from the table for herself and begins leafing calmly through it, as if unconcerned by their interaction.

'Did you say this booklet commemorates the way this impostor died, and describes how his soul and his excrement left his body at the same time in the bathroom?'

When nobody answers, he adds gloatingly, 'He died a shameful, ignominious death, inappropriate for somebody who claimed he'd come to guide the world to salvation. Anyway' – addressing himself to Huda – 'I don't think you'd be able to distinguish between what's true and what's false in his teaching, because you are ignorant of the Holy Quran and its interpretation.'

The Indian youth answers calmly, 'But, brother, neither the Holy Quran nor the prophetic traditions mention that a person who suffers from diarrhoea and meets his fate in the toilet has died a shameful death! Is he not, furthermore, a human being? Isn't it reasonable that a person gets rid of his food in the recognised manner?'

'First of all, I'm not your brother, and enough of this vulgarity! I'm afraid that soon you're going to force us to witness how you yourself get rid of your food.'

Huda hurries off and Yvonne follows her.

'Why did you follow me? I thought you wanted to tremble in his arms.'

'No, no, please. I don't want to tremble as he strangles me to death.'

'I'm trying to picture him being intimate with a woman but I can't.'

'He'd do whatever he wanted with her, to punish her because she'd agreed to be alone with him.'

'Let's teach him a lesson he won't forget.'

'I'm one hundred per cent ready, happy to kill him. And I've changed my mind. I don't want to find Tahir. I have the feeling that I'll fall in love with someone at the wedding.'

They walk along a path that is supposed to take them out of Hyde Park. Most of the paths have been blocked off and the grass is being subjected to a beautification exercise, according to the notice that apologises to visitors and promises that the park will be decked out in green again in the very near future.

The ground looks like the squares on a draughtboard. Each square has its own colour – from brown earth to yellow grass to a stagnant pool of water swarming with crows and pigeons who have come to investigate nothingness. Dogs run around playing together, pretending to fight, and the two women are back at Speakers' Corner again.

Huda sighs. 'Is it possible that we've come back to Speakers' Corner? Swear to me, Yvonne, that you're not guilty of bringing us back here on purpose for the sake of that Arab clown?'

'I swear on the Virgin Mary that I'm innocent. It must be Ta'abbata Sharran. He's never ever going to let us leave this place. He wants to have his revenge on us before we can teach him a lesson, and God has answered his prayers.'

'See how the Virgin Mary is in league with you,' remarks Huda, seeing Tahir in the first group of people, where an Egyptian tourist is chastising his Arab brothers in London for becoming too serious while those who live in the jaws of hell believe that, to quote the old saying, 'The worst disasters are the ones that make you laugh'. He tells them of a fatwa issued by a shaykh, who agreed that a youth who wanted to become a martyr in an original way by hiding explosives in his bottom could allow another man to have sex with him several times until his bottom grew wide enough, '… you know what I mean!'

So Tahir protests and assures the Egyptian tourist that the Arabs in London have their fair share of jokes and tells him the story of the Arab shaykh of a mosque who forbade the wearing of Nike sports shoes because the word means 'fuck' in Arabic, and forbade women to drive in case they damaged their ovaries; and there was a woman, yes a woman and not a shaykh, who wouldn't allow Muslim girls to sit on chairs or sofas because they would get too comfortable sitting like this and it would be easy for anybody, human or jinn, to have sex with them, especially jinns, as they are very fond of human women.

But the Egyptian insists that his stories are more amusing than the stories of the Arabs of London, and proceeds to recount the story of his cousin who suffered from erectile dysfunction while participating in the revolution against Mubarak, and the doctor prescribed sex films, provided the actors were Muslims.

While the bystanders laugh appreciatively, an Englishwoman in her late sixties remarks, 'This is the first time I've seen Arabs and Muslims laughing and joking, even about religious matters.'

This turns out to be tempting fate, as Ta'abbata Sharran descends on the Egyptian, threatening to stuff his mouth with cotton wool if he doesn't leave at once, so the Egyptian raises his hand in farewell: 'OK, never mind. Bye bye, London.'

'Have you noticed that Ta'abbata Sharran is like a ghost who appears as soon as he hears the word "Islam"?' comments Huda. 'It looks to me as if he goes around all the groups picking out his victims.'

'But where's Tahir gone?' responds Yvonne.

The bystanders disperse like swarms of bees to other groups, but the Englishwoman who praised the cheerful spirit of the Muslim debaters approaches Huda and asks her if she's Muslim, as she has a question for her.

She doesn't say yes or no when asked, 'Are you a Muslim?' For her the Quran is an amazing riddle, conversing with her, making her contemplate and marvel, scaring her, but also entertaining her like a good book. She loves the images, as if God is entering her heart via the figs and olives. She sees herself in vast fields among fig trees laden with delicious fruit and olive trees producing delectable olive oil. It's as if the Creator understood that the fanatics were going to destroy all of life's beauty, and in order to prove to them that feeling and imagination and the senses were all as important as the mind he said to them, 'By the fig and the olive and Mount Sinai and this safe city of Mecca ...'

She used to whisper, 'Oh Lord, how wonderful your language is. There's nothing like it.' So when she listened intently to the Quran being explained, either at home or in religious education classes at school, it seemed normal and ordinary, earthly rather than divine, as if it was telling stories about people in her neighbourhood, and she would apologise to the Quran and the Creator of mankind. As the days and years went by, her mind took her to another place, as far as could be from the Holy Book and the subject of religion. Her life went in a different direction and she would resort to silence rather than commenting on religious topics. But after the explosion of the twin towers in New York she was surprised how angry it made her when she saw religious leaders turning into monsters and relying on spurious theological arguments to defend themselves. She would rush to call devout relatives or family friends from Toronto, or even religious men who had known her father, urging them to form some kind of group with their peers, not only to express their repugnance at the barbaric crimes committed in the name of religion, but to officially condemn those who incited young people to become martyrs.

She went even further than that, writing to the Pakistani Taliban after they shot the student Malala because she had insisted on her right to be educated and urged all girls to do the same. In her letter to the Taliban, Huda wrote: 'Has it slipped your minds, you who wanted to kill Malala, that killing a human being is killing a person made in the image of the Creator? Can a believer allow himself the authority to eliminate another even if he disagrees with him?' She finished her letter off by saying, 'It seems that you have forgotten the Sura of the Blood Clot.' Then she quoted the first few lines of the sura: 'Read* in the name of your Lord, who created man from a blood clot, read in the name of your most generous Lord, who taught the use of the pen, taught man what he did not know ...' She wrote, 'The first thing that the Prophet's inspiration demanded of him was that he should read, not that he should pray or fast or give alms or do the pilgrimage or jihad, but that he should read and write with a pen and learn.'

She gave this letter to a Canadian friend who went on a visit to Pakistan. 'It's not important that the letter reaches the Taliban. Just put it in a post box and somebody's bound to read it.'

She signed the letter 'Huda, daughter of Shaykh So-and-So, who is proud of the father who encouraged her to study and absorb learning so that she could become a lawyer, although in the end she chose the theatre.'

In response to the Englishwoman's question, 'I was born to a Muslim family,' answers Huda.

'I'm Muslim and not Muslim, Arab and not Arab, and now I'm English,' teases Yvonne.

'I can see that you've become English by your hair and your accent,' the Englishwoman tells Yvonne.

As Huda smiles encouragingly at the Englishwoman, she sees Ta'abbata Sharran standing on a crate like the speakers. *He must have heard me saying that I was born to a Muslim family, and now he's getting ready to have his revenge on me.* Then she breathes a sigh of relief when she hears him announcing that a demonstration for Syria would take place in front of the American Embassy at three that afternoon.

---

*The word 'Read' here is ambiguous and is sometimes translated as 'Recite', but Huda, along with many others, prefers to interpret it as 'Read'.

'I have a neighbour who wears a burka,' complains the Englishwoman to Huda. 'I'm sorry to say that I'm scared each time I see her, and I only feel reassured when I hear her voice. Sometimes I think she might be a man! Maybe she's like the terrorist who managed to escape from a London mosque hiding behind a chador and burka, or the thieves who wear burkas and rob jewellers' shops! Anyway, my question is this: Is there a text in Islamic law that says women have to cover their faces?'

Huda answers sharply, 'Islam doesn't say that a Muslim woman has to wear a niqab or a burka. This is a heresy, otherwise you'd see all the Muslim women on the pilgrimage to Mecca with their faces covered. I remember the religious studies teacher at my school in Lebanon told us a nice story about the origin of the niqab. He said that the niqab wasn't known until a young girl from an Arab tribe covered her face when her father tried to marry her off to a man against her will, and in those days a woman couldn't go against her family's wishes.'

'Sorry, what period are we talking about?'

'The eighth century, and maybe this is still the case in some Arab and Muslim societies. The point is that this girl tried to convince her mother to take her side on the pretext that she was too young, but her mother refused to listen to her, and when the mother of the prospective bridegroom came to visit the girl's family, as was the custom, to see what she looked like, and confirm that she had reached puberty and would make a suitable wife for her son, the girl began to put her plan into action: she covered her face with a piece of black cloth that reached below her neck and had two small round holes for her eyes, and went into where her mother and the mother of the groom were waiting, and began dancing and rolling her eyes as if she had lost her mind. She snatched a cup of coffee from in front of the groom's mother and made as if to drink it and spilt it on her black face cover, at which point the mother of the groom took to her heels. When the girl's father heard of her trick, he swore that he would make her wear this black cloth for the rest of her life. News of the event went around the other tribes and as a result girls who wanted to refuse forced marriage resorted to the same strategy. Subsequently the niqab became a recognised tradition in the girl's tribe and with the passage of time it spread to the other tribes.'

The Englishwoman gasps in surprise. 'How strange! I wonder if women who wear the niqab today know this story?'

'I don't know,' answers Huda.

'Of course you don't know, because you're not from the nation of Muhammad, peace be upon him. This tale must be your own composition, a product of your imagination. I'm sure you invented it, but I'll look into it,' says Ta'abbata Sharran.

So he was behind her, following her, watching her, like her brother in Beirut, and exactly like the neighbour who tricked her father into coming to the beach to catch her wearing a swimsuit.

'What's the name of this tribe, wise philosopher?'

'It's none of your business. I'm talking to this woman. It's between me and her. I'm not giving a speech.'

But the group around Huda has begun to grow bigger.

'Naturally you're avoiding the answer because you don't know it.'

When she sees the smile of malicious delight on his face and senses the resentment coursing through him, she can't help saying in a superior tone: 'Ah, I forgot to mention the name of the girl's tribe. It's Matir,' and she looks at the man from the desert with a smile fierce as a dagger's blow. But he pays no attention to her reaction and replies sarcastically, 'You said before that it was the religious studies teacher who told you this fairy tale, but you didn't mention which religion! If you say it was Islam, then you're deluded, and you're not a true Muslim, for here you are with your head and face uncovered and arms bare.'

Huda had removed her light jacket, underneath which she wore a silk shirt with a low neckline, printed with birds of all shapes and colours, and skinny blue jeans.

'Ah, I also forgot to say that Islam does not oblige a Muslim woman to wear long dresses that drag on the ground. They were a product of the desert too and were the tribal girls' idea. They used to creep out to meet their lovers under cover of darkness, and in an effort to make sure that people didn't discover their footprints in the sand, they devised these long dresses that trailed over the sand and erased them.'

He interrupts her, moving closer to her: 'You've gone too far now. My patience has run out. I forbid you categorically to talk about Islam in this irresponsible way.'

Ignoring him, Huda continues: 'How I wish we could stop attaching so much importance to the niqab, when there are life-and-death issues like the marriage of under-age girls, some of them as young as eight. Girls like toy dolls, forced to become playthings themselves, and have intercourse with men old enough to be their fathers or grandfathers.'

The anger on the youth's face was terrifying as he said to her in formal Arabic: 'Do you know that hens are slaughtered if they cry like roosters?'

'What?'

'A hen – if she makes a noise like a male bird, she must be killed. Do you understand now?'

'I don't understand Arabic.'

'Are you threatening her?' shouts Yvonne in Arabic.

'Yes, I'm threatening her and you, and everybody who interferes in what doesn't concern them, for they'll hear things that they won't like.'

Huda looks at him as if she's dissecting him: he's a hypocrite, adopting a pious persona, and she feels she must expose him. The colour and cut of his olive trousers, his burgundy scarf, turquoise ring, silver bangles and sports shoes, his big eyes that appear to be rimmed in kohl and the way he wears his hair all suggest that he frequents clubs and dances with a glass of neat whisky in his hand, rather than telling his prayer beads and praying five times a day.

'Ooh, look at us. We're quaking in our boots,' replies Yvonne, pretending to tremble.

The Englishwoman joins in: 'What's going on? Is this all a result of my question about the niqab?'

Before anyone can answer her, Tahir comes up and says to Ta'abbata Sharran: 'Brother Hisham, you don't have the right to reward and punish. Only our Lord can do that. Didn't we agree on this last Sunday?' Then, turning to Huda, 'What's this fascinating information about the burka, Daughter of the Cedars? I think, my Lebanese sister, that the niqab is the first of the three tools of seduction. The second is a red dress and the third is kohl round the eyes.'

The elderly Englishman from earlier, leaning on his walking stick and puffing at a cigarette, calls out, 'I've got a question for the lady who talked about blacks and Islam,' but Hisham intervenes: 'No. You can't ask her a question because her information is spurious.'

'This is extremely unfortunate,' expostulates the Englishwoman. 'Dialogue is supposed to be of the essence at Speakers' Corner, however dissimilar the mentalities and

however fierce the clashes of opinion. We should understand that this tradition is a reflection of the democracy
that we enjoy here in Britain.'

Huda addresses the Englishman. 'What did you want
to ask?'

'Thanks. My question is the following: What happens
to women who wear niqabs on the day of resurrection
when they arise from their graves without niqabs?'

Huda starts to leave without answering, while Tahir
replies: 'The niqab wearers will unintentionally disobey
God, as instead of covering *that* – he points downwards –
'they'll be preoccupied with covering their faces.'

Hisham directs words at the Arab youth in a Maghrebi
accent as if he is spraying him with bullets, and the youth
replies, 'Do you know what my head told my tongue to
say? As long as you are my neighbour, I shall never know
peace.'

Hisham ignores him and says: 'We will rise up from
our long sleep without genitals and our bodies will be
covered in hair. Almighty God, who has made man to
perfection, will surely make the decaying bones live, and
resurrect him to perfection.'

Huda remembers that she asked exactly the same
question of her religious studies teacher, who answered
that the angels would cover our bodies, while her father
assured her that everyone would be too busy waking up
from death and coming back to life again to worry about
such things.

This time the two women move fast through the crowd
as they make for the exit, but Tahir calling to them stops
them in their tracks. 'Just a moment. Don't leave me
before I've had the chance to talk to you, it would kill me!'

'Shall we let him come with us if he wants to?'

'Where to? To the wedding?'

'We could invite him to have dinner with us tomorrow.'

Panting, he catches up with them. 'I want to thank you both. You're the best propaganda for Islam. A young woman like you' – turning to Huda – 'talking about the burka is more important than hundreds of speakers trying to convince the West that there are modern Muslim women, blonde ones with green eyes, and dark, sexy ones. I've got an idea: Why don't the three of us begin a dialogue with the title "Free Hugs with Muslims"? We allow everybody who wants to find out about Islam, men or women, to embrace us, then they might get a better understanding of how spontaneous and open we can be.'

'We're ready!' exclaims Yvonne.

They introduce themselves, and he carries on: 'Pleased to meet you, Huda and Yvonne, Yvonne and Huda.'

All of a sudden, Hisham appears, as if he has sprung from the bowels of the earth. Tahir smiles: 'Look who's come to apologise to you, ladies.' He turns to Hisham. 'I was just saying why don't the three of us begin a dialogue with the British. These two ladies wear black abayas and cover their heads, but wear masses of make-up, bright red lipstick, or better still wear niqabs, then raise their veils from time to time, and give hugs to the British. Can you imagine the reaction from the British men?'

'Shut up, you idiot. Shut up. I knew you were stupid, but I didn't know how stupid,' shouts Hisham.

'What's it to do with you? For your information, we're no longer at Speakers' Corner. This is a private meeting. Now, where was I, my dears? I know, I was saying can you imagine the sight of a veiled woman embracing a British man?'

Before he finishes his sentence, he is brought to the ground by a sudden powerful blow aimed at him by Hisham. Blood pours from Tahir's face. Yvonne bends over him, while Huda goes after Hisham, shouting, 'How can you be so violent? Aren't you ashamed of yourself? I'm calling the police.'

Yvonne calls, 'Huda, Huda.'

'And you're not worthy of your name.[*] Your name is innocent of you. What's the connection between you and the true faith? You're error[†] personified. And remember, your place is in the kitchen, not here.'

'Yes, my place is in the kitchen,' shouts Huda at the top of her voice, 'so I can make a soup from your bones.'

Thunderstruck at this response, Hisham merely shakes his head vindictively, chewing on his lip, and leaves the group at speed.

People immediately crowd around the young Arab, including the Jamaican with the Hitler moustache and Myrtle, who helps Tahir to his feet, wipes the blood from his face and wants to call an ambulance, but Tahir protests: 'It's not worth it. Otherwise the police will use this incident as an excuse to give us more grief. It's best if I leave quickly before someone calls them.'

'Why don't we take you home in a taxi?' suggests Yvonne.

'It's best if you give me the fare and I deal with it myself!' says Tahir. 'My grandfather always went on foot from our village to the town where his school was. One day when it was pouring with rain a man happened to pass by on a donkey and offered to give my grandfather a ride in exchange for ten piastres. My grandfather replied, "Why don't you give me five piastres and I'll give you and your donkey a lift on my back?"'

Everyone laughs and the Jamaican says, 'I'll walk with you to Marble Arch underground station. It's very close.'

---

[*] Huda: guidance on the right path; truth; the true religion.

[†] In Arabic 'dalal': straying from the right path; error.

Tahir begins to move around, leaning on the Jamaican, and nods a greeting to the others before leaving.

'Thank you, my friends. I'm so happy, in spite of all that's happened,' says Tahir. 'Something you hate can be good for you. I never imagined for a moment that Myrtle, queen of the racists, whom I've enjoyed teasing for the past four years, would volunteer to help, and the Nazi, king of the anti-British racists, that they'd actually compete with one another to help me. And there they are now shaking hands without being told! Look how they abandoned everything and rushed over to rescue me. As for you, my pretty Lebanese friends, I want to marry both of you.'

'Are you certain you don't want us to take you to the doctor?' asks Myrtle.

'No. No thanks. But do you know what? This coming Sunday I promise I won't criticise you or make fun of you.' The woman smiles affectionately at him, and he continues, 'But I'll make a hole in your tongue, like some Berber tribe does to brides on their wedding night, and put a ring in the hole and tie a thread to it and pull on it whenever I want to shut you up.'

Myrtle laughs heartily and says cheerfully to him, 'Now I'm sure you're fine. So I'll see you next Sunday.'

Yvonne and Huda kiss him on both cheeks by way of farewell. 'We'll see you next Sunday.'

'Indeed you will, my blonde and my brunette.'

They walk away.

'It's strange how I stopped fancying Tahir and just felt sorry for him as soon as I saw his face covered in blood.'

'What happened to him must have shocked him to the core. I wanted to ask him if Ta'abbata Sharran always fought with him, or if the fact that I was there provoked him. And now that nasty, stupid guy thinks he's escaped my clutches.' Huda extends her hands in front of her, claw-like, and bares her teeth, like a cat ready to pounce.

'Did you notice how he ran off like a rat abandoning ship?'

'But he won't escape from Error! Because I'm sure I'll come across him again at the American Embassy at 3 p.m. Big Ben time. Error will get the better of him sooner or later.'

'Oh, I forgot the demonstration.'

'Error never forgets.'

Huda stands in front of the advertising posters that Yvonne has designed inspired by certain scenes or situations in Lebanese life that she still remembers from her childhood: the poster of the Bedouin singer with full lips and kohl-rimmed eyes, the usual beauty spot on her cheek, and the caption 'My hair colour matches my beauty spot'; another of a man handing his wife a packet of pills, on which is written 'Meet my new friend. His name is Aspro.' Huda begins to hum the song from the old advert: 'Aspro, let it be your friend, Aspro, let it be your friend.'

Yvonne hurries out of her room, blusher in hand, to complete the song with her friend. 'Aspro removes aches and pains, Aspro, Aspro, Aspro.'

Another poster shows a mermaid with the face of a society woman known as the Lebanese Esther Williams because of her swimming prowess. Beneath her picture was the caption 'I use Mermaid tampons because they allow me to swim every day.'

'Wicked girl. I never saw this on your website.'

'It's fresh from the oven.'

'It's fantastic. I want you to design a poster for the play.'

Finally there is a poster that prompts Huda to declaim in a theatrical tone: 'Who said that a girl's honour is like a match you can only light once?' These words appear in Arabic, accompanied by an English translation, around an open white box in which lies a single strawberry, displayed like a piece of jewellery. Accompanying it also is an inscription that reads: 'Don't worry, girls, nobody will ever know your secret. You won't need a doctor to restore your virginity, or a pharmacist to sell it to you. The magic solution is to buy your virginity from this site: www.hongkongandsingapore.com.' Yvonne appears again with six packets in her hands. 'Please take one' – she opens one – 'if you want to be a virgin again! Go on.'

'No, no. I don't believe this!' shrieks Huda.

'You'd better believe it. Chinese hymens are bestsellers in the Arab world, especially in Egypt. They cost fifteen dollars a packet! The woman stuffs the "strawberry" up there and when the groom has sex with her it bursts and its juice flows like crimson blood and the man has peace of mind because his bride is a virgin! My poor auntie, she became a nun and married the church because her fiancé deflowered her before he went to work in Brazil, to make sure she wouldn't think of marrying anyone else. But unfortunately he never sent for her and she never heard from him again so she took refuge with the church.'

A wicked thought flashes through Huda's mind.

'If your aunt had been living in our poor quarter in Beirut, our neighbour Saadiyya would have given her powdered glass and shown her how to put it "up there" on her wedding night, so she'd have bled like a virgin who'd never kissed anyone but her mother. Long live China! Yvonne, you're a genius! The poster is super amazing!'

*

A year after her father's death, Huda had decided that she would become a man, as males are both kings and ghouls. You're not allowed to eat in front of them, or meet their eyes. You have to cover your knees so the walls don't see them, because maybe men's eyes are somehow left in the walls, for men are present even when they are absent. You mustn't stand on the balcony and look out at the world. You mustn't talk on the phone.

That night Huda cut her hair herself. *I want to be a man!* Men are kings and ghouls. Men don't cover themselves, or the only one who did was the neighbours' son who liked his own sex and whose father sent him to the shaykh, Huda's father, so that he could help him banish devilish temptation and make him once again as God had created him, a man who loved women. 'But God made me like men in spite of myself.' 'No, son,' replied the shaykh. 'God created human beings in pairs so that the human race would continue.' After a few months of receiving advice and being exposed to some scare tactics, the young man confided to Huda's father that he had definitely repented and that all he wanted now was to carry out the five religious duties and spare himself evil in the next life, and the first thing he needed to do was to cover himself!

Huda's short hair, her eyes free of kohl or eyeshadow, her unplucked eyebrows and bare skin, made some of the young women become infatuated with her, while the local youths thought she was competing with them for the women and remarked when they saw her: 'Do you dress to the right or the left, for we can't see it at all?'

She changed her mind. She didn't want to be male or female. She wanted to be a car so she could travel through the streets in broad daylight or the depths of the night with only freedom as her companion. She learnt to drive in secret, surprising her instructor with her skill. She told him of her desire to teach women to drive, in particular covered women who wouldn't accept instruction from a man. The owner of the driving school agreed, laughing and nodding his head in pleasure at the idea, and wrote on the car, 'Ladies Taught By a Female Instructor'. She reverted to wearing a headscarf so that the covered women would trust her, and taught them not to be afraid, to have confidence in themselves and not care about what men said: 'Where are they driving to? Hell, or Qadisha Valley? Hey sister, you know cars run on petrol, not tomato sauce!'

When she decided to join her brother in Toronto, some years after the outbreak of war, and enrol in college to study theatre, she was eager to carry on teaching Arab women in Toronto to drive in her spare time, but as soon as she arrived there she encountered the old Huda again and the proof was that when she met her college lecturer, she became infatuated with the way he spoke, the stories he told and his theories of life. She fell in love with his fingers holding a CD, his smile when she came to his office in the university one day to ask him if he had looked at the essay she had handed in the day before, because she wanted to change something in it. As he looked for her paper, he chatted away, recounting how he had been distracted when he was teaching the previous day, and had begun describing a play he had attended, and the long dinner afterwards, where he had drunk a lot of wine. He gave her the essay. She stood up quickly, thanking him, promising to return it the next morning. When she reached the door he called to her: 'I'm really curious to know what you're going to change in your essay. Can I make a copy of it before you put in the changes?'

She handed him her essay and he fed the pages into the photocopier and promised her he wouldn't read it before she gave him the corrected copy. She had chosen a story from a Schubert song as the assignment was to create a theatrical situation derived from another art form: a painting, a novel, a piece of music, some verses of poetry. The theatrical situation she had chosen was 'the unknown': it was the tale of a dwarf and a queen who were alone in a boat. She had relied on the booklet accompanying the CD, which told the story.

A queen and her dwarf were alone in a boat that was being tossed about by the waves and carried far out to sea, until the mountains looked like ghostly shapes shrouded in mist. Why had the two of them set out on this boat trip? Was it because the queen was fed up with life and wanted an adventure? Had the weather suddenly changed? But while Huda was leafing through the booklet again the following day, she noticed that the rest of the story of the song was on the next page. The dwarf was the one who had taken the queen on this sea trip in order to strangle her with a red silk cord because she had chosen the king over him.

When her professor praised her a few days later for her treatment of the subject, she invited him to dinner. The third time they met, she said she'd like to visit him in his flat. She confessed to him that she felt seriously confused and wanted to free herself from this feeling, then surprised herself by undoing her skirt and sitting in front of him in her tights, then taking off her tights and sitting there in her knickers. Now the professor was confused and tried to avoid looking at her, but smiled and asked if she would like something to drink. He wanted to know more about her.

'Did you tell me you were from Lebanon? From a Muslim family?'

She didn't answer him. She was still under the tormenting effect of the red chilli pepper, of Fatima tied to the door handle, Nadira and her fainting fit, Issam imitating a monkey, Sawsan going up into the air, her face to the sky, calling, 'I'm the wasp', and Huda, looking down at the ground, calling, 'I'm the bee'.

She took off her knickers in front of the Canadian professor. 'I know that this is what we're both thinking about, and if you're not thinking about it yet, then maybe in five minutes.'

When he mounted her and she screamed in pain, the professor continued to move up and down on top of her, only stopping when she shouted, 'Please, you're hurting me, and I'm a virgin.'

At this, he jumped like a mouse caught in a trap, and when he saw the blood on himself and on the sofa, he yelled, 'What's this? A bloodbath?'

Inwardly dancing for joy because she had got rid of her virginity, she answered silently, 'Yes, *Macbeth* for ever!'

'So what have you decided? Will you come to the wedding reception with me after all?'

'And lose my big chance to have my revenge on Ta'abbata Sharran?' answers Huda, patting the strawberry in its packet in her handbag.

They leave the house at the same time, Yvonne in her car and Huda hurrying on foot in the direction of the American Embassy, a tremendous enthusiasm to have her revenge on Ta'abbata Sharran making her heart beat faster.

But she begins to walk more hesitantly, her feet reluctant to obey her. She urges herself on in an audible voice, 'Come on, Huda, come on,' reminding herself of what he'd said to her: 'A hen – if she makes a noise like a male bird, she must be killed,' recalling his frowning face as he threatened her: 'Do you understand now?'

Instead of rekindling the fires of revenge, these thoughts make her shudder. He's vicious, frightening, like a pre-programmed robot. But she doesn't stop, doesn't turn back, and hurries on her way, her phone in her hand guiding her to the American Embassy.

The commotion of the demonstrators in front of the American Embassy, their shouting drowning out the roar of the traffic. Police everywhere. Women with and without veils. Women wearing headscarves, with and without children. Men with beards and men without beards. *Allahu akbar, Allahu akbar.* Their voices echoing round the square make the pigeons fly here and there, and like the pigeons she is uncertain what she should do.

But who are these protestors? The original opposition or other extremist groups?

She feels like an impostor among them. She is supposed to blend in with them or pretend to be sympathetic to the slogans they are chanting. Should she shout with those calling for Asad to be punished, or with those crying '*Allahu akbar*'? She tries to find Ta'abbata Sharran without success and walks away across Grosvenor Square. From there she can see the Canadian flag flapping above a white old-style building. Her heart flutters at the sight of it, for these days it has taken the place of the Lebanese flag, which used to make her want to cry when she first lived abroad.

She returns to the demonstration, indifferent to the fact that she might arouse suspicion. She tries to lose herself among the crowds as she searches for the tallest figure there, for Hisham, and actually catches sight of him beating his hand in the air as if wishing he had magic powers and could smash the embassy windows and wreak havoc on the records and documents inside.

Huda waits for the protests to end and the demonstrators to leave. A girl wearing a headscarf smiles at her and she wonders whether to ask her when the event will be over, but decides against it. The time passes quickly, consumed mainly by people shouting, while others eat the sweets and sandwiches they've brought with them, or exchange mobile numbers and take selfies. She keeps her eyes on the beautiful brown face that picked a fight with her that morning, and as soon as she sees him leaving the demonstration she follows him, walking fast at times, slowly at others, crossing the street to the opposite pavement, jostling people, dawdling, trying to keep out of sight. Then she sees him standing at a bus stop in Oxford Street and waits five minutes before approaching it. She tries to read the notice to find out where the buses are bound. Suddenly she clutches the bus stop with one hand and her head with the other, pretending to feel dizzy and weak all of a sudden, then clinging to an Englishwoman in the queue. Hands reach out to catch her. She begins to talk incoherently in Arabic: 'Oh God, I'm going to die, oh God.'

'We can't understand what you're saying! Sorry, can you talk to us in English? We want to help you,' says the Englishwoman. Huda opens her eyes as if semi-conscious, and when she notices that among those trying to help her is the dark-skinned youth, she stares at him in mock surprise and terror.

'Please can one of you call an ambulance?' requests the woman and Ta'abbata Sharran volunteers: 'I will.' Then he says to Huda in Arabic, 'I'm going to call an ambulance for you.'

'No, no, please, there's no need. I feel better. I don't want them to take me to hospital.'

As soon as he translates Huda's words to those gathered around her, they disperse, realising that the two of them speak the same language. Huda neither expresses her gratitude to him nor rebuffs him, for she is still supposedly only half conscious.

'I almost fainted, I don't know why. I must contact my friend.'

With some trouble she takes out her phone and struggles even more to find the number, before leaving a message in a soft, weak voice: 'This is Huda. I've forgotten the key. I don't feel well. Please call me as soon as you get this.' Then she says, 'My friend's not at home. I need to sit down for a bit. Could you help me get to a café?'

'Shall I take you to a doctor?'

'I feel better. I just want to drink some water and rest a little.'

'Come with me.' He doesn't hail a taxi, although he asks her if she is all right to walk. They walk along together quite naturally, almost as if they hadn't detested each other not long before.

They arrive at a Starbucks at the beginning of Oxford Street and as soon as he finds an empty table, Huda promptly sits down while he remains standing without uttering a word, as if suddenly remembering that he hates her.

'Goodbye.'

'Thank you. Thank you very much. I've put you to a lot of trouble. I'm sorry!'

'It's nothing.'

'Goodbye. Thanks again.'

She lets him take a few steps then calls out: 'Brother, excuse me! Can I buy you a coffee or a tea?'

'No, thank you, there's no need for that.'

'I know, but please.'

'I have to get back to work.'

'OK, sorry. I thought you wouldn't be working on a Sunday. I … I feel so tired.' Her voice trembles as if she is on the point of tears. 'I want to lie down and my friend hasn't called me back yet.' And she begins to cry.

'Why don't you call another friend?'

'I don't know anyone here. I live in Canada. Will you do me a favour and get me a cup of tea?' She hands him a five-pound note and asks him to get himself something to drink too, so he takes the money and goes over to the counter. She follows him with her eyes and observes him as he stands in the queue waiting his turn. *Where can we be alone together?* she says to herself. *Does he live on his own? I wonder what he does for a living and why he works on Sundays. Who is he?* He returns almost at once with one tea and gives her the change. 'I'm late for work.'

When she puts a hand to her head and sighs profoundly, he says, 'Shall I take you to the house of a friend of mine? His wife is very nice.'

'Does she have children?'

'Yes. They're very well-behaved and they won't bother you.'

'No, I'm not bothered for myself, but I'm afraid they might catch something. Maybe I'm getting flu.' She feels her forehead.

He looks at his watch. 'Sorry, I'm late. I have to go.'

'Thank you so much. Goodbye.' She bows her head and starts crying again.

Ignoring her tears, he takes a couple of steps away from the table. Out of the corner of her eye she sees him looking at her, so she cries more energetically, until he comes back towards her.

'Come with me. Don't worry, you can trust me, sister. You'll be fine.'

Crying more violently than ever, she mutters, 'You're so decent, brother, so decent.'

She gets to her feet with his help and they walk along together and take the bus. She doesn't ask him where he's taking her. He must have been lying when he said he worked on a Sunday. He lets her pay her own fare. When she gets off the bus, she catches herself walking more briskly and slackens her pace, stops briefly and then sets off again, breathing heavily. He leads the way to a block of flats whose cast-iron front door has glass inlaid with gold filigree. She is impressed, even if this is a friend's flat, but just as she is telling herself that unemployment certainly wasn't the reason for his emigrating here, nor poverty the cause of his fanaticism, he opens the door and says, 'I'm a porter in this building.' She's not that bothered by this revelation, remembering her relationship with a musician in Canada who worked as a porter in an apartment block from time to time and used to raid the bottles of wine stored in the basement by one of the building's inhabitants.

It is a noble old building: lights sparkling from a crystal chandelier, a gilded mirror and two chairs round a beautiful fireplace. They approach the other porter who is sitting in a small room next to the lift, and Hisham addresses him: 'I'm sorry, I've kept you waiting, but this sister was a little unwell and she was alone and couldn't find her friend. She's a stranger in London, visiting from Canada. I'll put her in our sitting room for a while.'

'Of course, of course,' answers the porter in an Irish accent.

Hisham takes her to the floor below where the carpet is grey, mouse-coloured, in contrast to the luxurious, green-and rose-coloured carpet in the entrance hall. Everything is grey, including the walls and the plastic tiles. They come to a large room containing a couch the colour of a rat that has never seen the light of day, a small television, a kettle and a microwave.

'You can rest on the couch here, sister. Nobody will bother you. Would you like a cup of tea?'

'If you don't mind!'

She closes her eyes, listening intently to every sound he makes. He is the soul of piety and seriousness, rigid as a steel box. She doesn't stand the slightest chance of piercing his armour. *I must leave once I've drunk the tea,* she thinks to herself.

'Here's the tea. You can stay here as long as you like. Nobody will bother you.'

The cup of tea whispers to her that she should get up and leave at once, not because it's cheap, nasty tea, but because Hisham has surprised her with his compassion, his humanity, his sense of duty towards her as a Muslim woman. In a roundabout way, he has apologised to her for his behaviour towards her that morning.

What, him, compassionate and humane? No, this couldn't be further from the truth. It's because he's seeing me in a weak state, thinks I've come down off my high horse. This honourable behaviour is just him getting tougher so that he can punish me more severely, to prove to me what an infidel I am, and how tolerance is a big deal in his religion.

She stretches out on the couch. The sounds of feet passing by on the pavement above reverberate in the room. The noise inside the building and outside in the street is never-ending. Toilets flushing, baths being run, water tanks gurgling, ventilation systems humming, as if all the floors in the building are bombarding the basement with their troubles. She hears people going up and down the stairs and even a cook complaining about having to prepare the same meal every day for the old lady who employs him.

An hour passes, in the course of which a maid comes in and makes herself a cup of coffee, sits on a chair to drink it, then leaves the room as if Huda isn't there. When Hisham doesn't return, she is convinced that it won't occur to him to check up on her. She gets up and ascends the few stairs to the porters' office and sees him sitting alone in the little room reading an engineering textbook in English. Could he be manufacturing a bomb?

'Are you leaving?'

'My friend called to say she wouldn't be home before midnight. I'm still not well actually. Do you know a small hotel that would let me have a room for a few hours, and also do you know a private doctor you could take me to?'

'I recommend cupping. There's someone who does it and I have the address. You can take the bus there. Or if you wish, I can order you a minicab. They're cheaper than black cabs.'

'What did you say? What's cupping?'

He looks online and tells her to read the page, so she bends her head, deliberately bringing it close to his, and he jumps up and moves away from her. She reads a couple of sentences and can't understand what they say until she sees a picture of 'air cups'.

'Ah, I know them, they're air cups. My mother used to put them on my back when I had a cold or bronchitis. I was scared of them.' She clasps her arms to her chest like a little girl. 'My mother would set fire to a cotton rag and put it directly inside the cup, then put it on my back.' She moves closer to the computer and reads, 'It is an authentic practice of the Prophet and even the angels recommend it.'

She doesn't say that she finds the contradiction between the technology of the computer and the description of cupping on its screen quite incredible.

'I can't believe they're still doing it. No, no, I'm not going to try it. I'm terrified to death of it.'

'If you put your trust in God, you won't be afraid of anything in this world and nothing bad will happen to you. Say, nothing will affect us except what God has decreed for us.'

'I don't know what's happened to me. This morning I was very healthy and energetic. Now all I want to do is lie down and sleep. Please take me to a cheap hotel where I can get a room and wait for my friend to come home.'

'Come along, sister. I'll take you to my own room. I won't need it for a few hours, after my shift ends.'

Fantastic. Visible progress. She's moving in on him, even if it's through the eye of a needle.

'Thanks, brother. Are you sure? I don't want to bother you. God has sent you to rescue me. It must be in response to my mother's prayers. Shall we take a taxi?'

'God the Almighty, the Most High,' he corrects her, then continues, 'I live here. Wait while I lock the door of the building.'

He takes her down to the basement again and leads her along another corridor to his room. He opens the door and she smells a musty odour mixed with insecticide and cleaning products. In the room are a chair, a bed and a table piled with Arabic books, and on a low shelf packets of pasta and rice and tins of tomato puree. He opens a cupboard and takes out a blanket, old but clean, that he spreads on the bed.

'God willing you'll feel better here, sister. There is no god but God.'

She doesn't respond as she should: 'And Muhammad is His messenger.'

She lies down. She wants him to see her lying on his bed in her top with the birds on it, a pattern that brings joy to the severe room, and her tight jeans that help her bottom look higher. She's taken off her shoes and socks, revealing deep red toenails. She puts a hand on her head, displaying an armpit, knowing that armpits can be provocative, reminiscent of the pubes, even when they're shaved. But he doesn't look at her, and goes out, closing the door behind him. She puts her tired feet on the pillow, for they need rest more than her head. After a while she gets up and begins inspecting his things, in case she comes across some alcohol or anything inconsistent with his rigid fanaticism, anything to expose him.

His room reminds her of some of her relatives' rooms, even her father's room when she sees the Quran and books of the prophetic traditions arranged on the table. There's a poster for an exhibition of the hajj where the Kaaba appears like a square black pupil in the white of the eye, and people praying or walking around it are like the veins in the eye. She reads 'Hajj: Journey to the Heart of Islam' and there is a comment, perhaps written by him, 'An exhibition on the hajj in the heart of the British Museum. How I wish the exhibition extended throughout the museum.'

The Holy Quran and a photo of the Kaaba still dominated the living room in their house in Beirut. During her last visit to Lebanon two years ago, she had noticed, under the glass of the tabletop, the graduation photo that she had sent to her mother from Toronto, alongside a photo of her father in his abaya and turban, and her brother holding a big fish that he had just caught. She remembers how her photo had urged her to be patient, reassuring her that she would be returning to Canada in a few days, and that there was no chance her childhood home would risk kidnapping her and imprisoning her against her will. She couldn't take her mother constantly asking her why she wasn't married yet. Now, in this religious man's room, she finds herself answering her mother: *Perhaps I shall never marry at all. And for your information I'm living next door to the Devil now.* Her mother used to mutter, 'In the Name of God the Compassionate the Merciful' whenever she saw workers digging deep beneath the roads of Beirut. 'Aren't they scared that they'll dig right down to the Devil?'

Huda remembers the time she said to her religious studies teacher at school in Lebanon, 'I don't understand, sir. Why do we actually let the Devil threaten us and get into our minds and tempt us to do bad things? Why are we scared of him from the day we are born till the day we die? Why didn't our Lord wipe him off the face of the earth from the beginning, the moment he rebelled?'

The teacher answered: 'Of course, my child, the Creator could have destroyed Satan in a moment, but God wants to test us to find out whose faith is strong.'

She replied, 'But I don't understand, sir, why there are all these complications. God doesn't need the approval and love of His creatures. They are the ones who need His approval and affection and we know that God and not Satan created heaven and earth, so the rivalry between God and Satan isn't logical.'

With the passing of time, the Devil took on a different aspect in Huda's mind. He no longer had an actual face or fiery eyes that emitted sparks. He became a phenomenon, or rather a manifestation of a state of indecision, like looking at the sky and wondering whether or not to take an umbrella.

But don't be afraid, mother. The Devil has run off to escape the prayers of the devout young man in whose room I am at this moment, by the way. And I can imagine that if you knew this young man, you would think he'd make a suitable husband for me. You'd say, 'He is God-fearing and upright.' I want to tell you why I'm not married yet. I'm a seagull, alighting for a moment then flying off, fishing in one stretch of water after another. My independence scares them. I always take the initiative. I'm the one in the driving seat. Of course, you won't understand what I mean by that. I'm going to tell you a story and I really hope you'll be able to understand. When a man took hold of me by the neck, trying to make me go down on him, down there, I head-butted him like a billy goat. And I'm pointing the finger of blame at you. I accuse you and my father of trying to suck the life out of me, and you especially.

The feelings of the past: violence and moral rectitude, violence mixed with affection and melancholy, to which she was a witness in spite of herself; her parents' abstemiousness in this life, and their longing for the next life, to the extent that when her father was enjoying eating spinach pastries, he used to say to her mother, 'They are as good as if the houris in Paradise prepared them and the angels brought them to us!'

Huda remembers being fascinated by the neighbours' peacock, how she took to standing in front of it for hours, feeding it bread and chickpeas, until her mother said, 'The peacock in Paradise is much more beautiful than the neighbours' peacock. Its tail is like an endlessly flowing river.'

The religious studies teacher described life in Paradise to his pupils: 'No work, no hardship; no sickness, pain or poverty; a life of comfort and ease, delicious food and lemonade on tap, lots of restaurants and the smell of kebabs wafting through the air; men sitting with houris under trees, watched by stars pale and bright, not to mention the waterfalls of wine cascading down.'

She used to say to herself, *Why is almost everything allowed in Paradise, and forbidden and taboo on earth! And the biggest bargains ever are in heaven, so no expensive weddings, no rent to pay or washing machines to buy and no midwives' fees, school fees or medical costs. Everyone is equal. So will Japanese people there understand me when I speak, and will I understand Russian?*

She put her hand up, aged thirteen, and asked the teacher: 'If the houris are the men's reward, what about the women, sir?' 'Rest,' answered the teacher. 'Their reward is rest, daughter, peace of mind and rest for the body and the soul. They will not be responsible for anything. They will lie in the gardens of Paradise and all varieties of fruit will hang from the trees and they won't even have to stand up to pick them. They won't have to do the laundry or wash the dishes, iron the clothes or cook or hoover. In short, my little daughter, in Paradise a woman will be a princess.'

She told him she didn't think her aunt would allow her uncle to sit with a houri because she was very jealous. The teacher nearly burst out laughing, but he controlled himself and replied, smiling, 'Your aunt will grow slimmer and more beautiful in paradise and become a strong, slender, charming young woman again, with skin as smooth as marble.'

She wasn't convinced by what he said, for God knows everything and He knows that there are a lot of people praying and fasting and following His commands in order to enter Paradise rather than hellfire, so their obedience to God is based on their fear for themselves; that is, on selfishness and hypocrisy. The whole human race should follow the example of the Sufi poet, Rabia al-Adawiyya, who said, 'When I die, I will set Paradise on fire and pour water into Hell, so Heaven and Hell will no longer be reasons for people to worship God.'

All of it made her lie awake thinking confused thoughts, and feel indolent and apathetic in the daytime. Some days she stayed away from school and spent the time in the vegetable markets, or in the meat markets watching the chicken and fish being sold, then went home as if she had been at school all day. When that started to happen frequently, the head teacher asked to see her father. Huda lied and claimed it was her father who stopped her going to school and that she was there today without him knowing, because he had gone on a trip outside Beirut. The truth was that Huda had come to school that day because she missed the pigeons on the roof of the house next door to the school, and the pigeon fancier calling each of them by name: Taj al-'Arus, Malikat Saba, Umm Kulthum. Huda continued to fabricate numerous excuses and lies about how busy her father was and why he was unable to come to the school to meet the head teacher, until finally the head teacher decided to visit Huda's house herself. At this point, Huda gave in and was honest with her: 'Why should I bother to waste my time studying in this life, when I'm supposed to focus on the next life, like my parents?' The head teacher, whose family came from Iran, understood Huda's excuse and began to warm to her and walk her home from school most days, since Huda's home wasn't far from the school. On the way, she bought her candy floss and pistachios and talked to her about Sufism and Sufis. One thing she said stuck in Huda's mind, a phrase that the head teacher urged Huda to repeat to her parents: 'Those who are abstemious in this life for fear of punishment are like incense, giving off the sweetest, purest fragrances when lit, then ending up as smoke and ashes.'

When I was born ... says Huda to herself, looking at the artificial flowers in a Nescafé jar in Hisham's room, *I was glowing, not dark and gloomy like my parents, because I wasn't nourished on their words, but on the fresh air filtered by my lungs. All the same, their blood ran through my brain*

*and heart and eyes. Then, as time went by, instead of cling-
ing on to them, I learnt to confront them, a separate human
being, not joined to them by anything more than the love
we exchanged, which I only gleaned from a word here and
there or from seeing the care with which food was prepared
for me.*

How can one person think for another? How could they
have expected her to surrender her mind to them? Yet she
was still sometimes in doubt when she heard sayings in
her childhood like 'Love of life is a sin'; 'Your body must
remain out of sight in the dark shadow of clothes so that
the sun does not stain it.'

'My daughter is sinful and dresses in an immoral way
and I am a religious man who gives spiritual guidance
to others,' wailed her father tearfully, while her mother
tried to sniff out the smell of the sea on her daughter.
Meanwhile Huda only had to put her head on the pillow
to feel the earth whirling her around, showing her the
North Pole, Eskimos in their igloos, the skyscrapers of
New York, and the house in China belonging to the characters from the novel *The Good Earth*. And only in bed
did Huda sing the song that for some reason her mother
had objected to the neighbours' girls singing: 'I'm thirsty,
lads, show me the way.'

Strange how her pious, conservative mother had agreed
to her going to Canada, to the unknown, without it occur-
ring to her that there Huda would be completely free with
no one to keep an eye on her, sleeping with anybody she
wanted! And how she thought her brother would be with
her day and night, as if he was his sister's guardian, even
though there was an hour and a half's train ride between
them.

When schools and colleges closed their doors in the
clamour of the civil war, it was her mother who borrowed

money to send her to Canada so that she could complete her education: 'That's what your father would have wished. He believed that girls should be educated just like men. He wanted you to become important: a lawyer or a political adviser, like in the days of the Prophet, peace be upon him.'

How often her father had defended Huda when her mother screamed at her and threatened her, forcing her to help with the housework. He used to say, 'Let her focus on her studies. Let her immerse herself in the treasures of knowledge and learning. School is more important for her now than domestic duties. Let her safeguard her future.'

Huda used to think that the war had taken place, harvesting the souls of the young men, the kidnap victims, the fighters, for her sake, so that everyone would forget that she had caused her father's death. Then she had changed her mind, for war is war. She was afraid of it, afraid of the shrapnel. Death was around her, searching for new victims every day. The neighbours' son, Hassan, went to his aunt's house to fetch a dress for his mother and on his way home he was struck by a piece of shrapnel and died on the spot. The same thing with the greengrocer, their neighbour and her children, and her brother's friend.

In peacetime, when the butcher slaughtered a chicken, she used to feel sad to see it flapping around in terror with the blood spouting from its neck, or rolling in the earth in the garden or running down the street with the children after it. Huda wished she could pick it up and hold it in her arms, but she had to make do with writing in chalk on the ground at the spot where the chicken had finally expired, 'The tree of forgetfulness does not grow where blood flows', a phrase she had learnt at school that stuck in her mind.

Isn't it strange that Hisham told her that the hens who cry like roosters should be slaughtered, and here's the hen now, lying in the rooster's coop that he himself opened for her!

Huda hears a knock at the door. She wakes up abruptly from a deep sleep, still suffering from jet lag. She sees Hisham standing some distance away in the corridor.

'Sorry if I've kept you waiting. I was fast asleep. Give me a few moments and I'll be gone.'

'Has your friend come home?'

'I told you before that she won't be back before midnight, but I'll leave anyway. Thanks. I'll never forget how kind you've been.'

'Thanks is due to God alone. We should all be charitable.'

She hurriedly picks up her bag from the chair and sits on the bed to fasten her shoes, while he waits outside. She puts on her jacket and comes out into the corridor.

'Thank you for everything. Goodbye.'

'Goodbye.' He goes into his room and closes the door.

After a few steps she turns back and knocks on his door. 'My phone. I think I may have left it here.' She enters the room in a leisurely way, removes the blanket from the bed with deliberate movements, slowly stands upright again. 'I'll take the blanket with me to wash it, then I'll bring it back to you.'

'No. There's no need for that.'

When she doesn't find the phone, she bends down to look under the bed, consciously remaining in that position for some time.

'What's your number? I'll call it.'

'I don't know. I bought it here in London and I haven't learnt it yet.'

He searches with her, muttering, 'In the Name of God' exactly like her mother and father used to do, the difference being that they quickly found whatever they'd lost, completely trusting that God would respond to their prayers, she thought.

'Did you go to the bathroom?'

Huda claps a hand to her head, feigning embarrassment, and hurries to the bathroom, waiting inside for a few moments before exclaiming petulantly, 'God, what have I done to deserve this?' Then in a louder voice, 'God help me. Help me, Lord.' And she breaks into a fit of sobbing that rises to a wail.

He asks her to make less noise in case people hear and think she's being attacked. Hastily she opens the virginity pack, looking at it and whispering, 'Come on, help me become a virgin again so he loses his mind,' and pushes the strawberry up between her legs. She puts the empty packet in her bag then changes her mind, opens the window and puts it on the outside window ledge, but doesn't emerge from the bathroom until he whispers, 'Sister Huda, sister Huda.' When he sees that she is still sobbing loudly, he asks her to come back into his room, placing a finger on his lips to indicate that she should calm down.

'I don't know what's happened to me. Since I went to Speakers' Corner this morning, I've had nothing but problems. First there was the crow that dropped its filth on me, then you shouted in my face and insulted me. I lost thirty pounds in the restaurant, left my key at home, the friend you saw with me didn't take me to Oxford like she promised. Then I had a dizzy spell and fainted in front of you at the bus stop, and now I've lost my phone. I can't take it any more.'

She flings herself at him, sobbing noisily, and the more vigorously he tries to fend her off, the more tightly she clings to him. She feels the vein in his neck throbbing violently even as he wriggles to free himself from her. When he finally manages to push her away, he says with some irritation, 'Please control yourself, sister.'

'Do you think I have a self to control? I feel that I'm nothing, that my self has abandoned me, I feel ...'

'You must be in this state because of the bad thoughts I had about you this morning when I was so angry with you. Forgive me, Lord.' Then raising his voice, 'Forgive me, sister.'

You think you're so pious. Let's see how pious you are in a minute, she thought.

Out loud she said in as weak and feeble a voice as she could muster, 'God must have responded to these thoughts of yours because you're so devout and He wanted to teach me a lesson. Sorry, I meant to say Almighty God. Please forgive me so that I can be free of this evil that pursues me.' She lunges at him like a bloodsucking mosquito, then flings her arms around him, clinging to him, holding him tight in both arms. She can hear his heart beating.

'Sister, sister.' He pushes her off him. 'What you're doing is haram. It goes against our true religion. You're spoiling my ablutions and my prayers and making me fall into sin.'

'But God Almighty knows that my intentions are pure. And deeds are judged by their intentions, aren't they?'

His voice takes on a warning note as if he is at Speakers' Corner: 'Have you gone mad? I don't care about intentions. What you're doing is completely wrong. Please, I don't want to regret my good deed. You must chase the Devil away.'

'Sorry, sorry,' she mumbles, staring at the ceiling.

Then she catches him off guard and throws herself at him again and holds him tight, saying, 'Sorry, brother. Don't be angry with me.'

He disengages himself from her, raising his hands heavenwards and saying in a loud voice, 'Forgive me, Lord. There is no power or strength save in Almighty God.'

He rushes to the window, opening it violently as if he is a prisoner, calling for God's help, asking to be rescued from his tribulations. But only the noise of the cars and the roar of the city surge into the room. He clutches his head, muttering, 'God protect me from the Devil. Control yourself, Hisham. Haste is the Devil's work. Slow down. You'll regret it. You'll become the lowest of the low. The hereafter lasts longer than fleeting pleasure!'

He punches the wall, the fridge door, the opposite wall, trying to calm himself down and relieve his agitation, while Huda stands there in amazement as if she's watching a scene from a play, stranger than any she's ever witnessed. Although she expected him to reject her advances, she hadn't imagined his resistance would be so frenzied and finds her eagerness to seduce him growing, the more he resists. He moves violently away from her, waving his hands around in the air like a helicopter's propeller to prevent her coming near him.

'I'm really sorry, brother Hisham. Trust me, I didn't mean what … In any case, I'm going, and if you come across my phone please throw it in the rubbish bin.'

She opens the door, pretending to leave, but is surprised to find two maids wearing blue overalls trying to drag a heavy carpet along the corridor, making it impossible for her to pass.

'We've caught you in the act. Trying to steal the carpet, were you?' jokes Hisham. Then he introduces Huda to them: 'This is my sister Huda.' He looks at Huda. 'Ah, I forgot something. Come back in.'

She follows him, suddenly cheerful. 'I thought Muslims didn't lie or dissemble, "Brother"!'

'I didn't lie. You really are my sister in religion. And this is why we triumphed over Satan when he tried to tempt us and lead us astray. Thank God, we blocked his path.'

'I thought you misunderstood me, or thought badly of me. It's true I held you close, but I had no impure feelings. I just needed to be reassured and to feel safe, nothing else, trust me. Anyway, I'm so happy you consider me your sister in religion and a true Muslim.'

He doesn't reply, his face remaining expressionless, so she makes as if to leave.

'Never mind. I must go now, to make sure the Devil leaves the building!'

'Please don't make fun of me. I have good intentions towards you. Will you marry me?' He frowns as he speaks, evidently expecting a quick answer.

'Did you really say what I think you said?'

'Yes. Will you marry me?'

Completely taken aback, she has no idea how to reply. Rather than 'You must be out of your mind', she answers, 'My father was a religious man, and he hoped I'd marry a pious and decent young man. He always used to say to me, "Don't fear those who fear the Lord!" Perhaps you would have been the ideal husband for me in his eyes. But I'm sorry, I'm not thinking of marriage at present.' She takes a deep breath before continuing, 'And also, we don't know each other. You don't know me nearly well enough to marry me!'

'What I do know is that I find you very attractive. Let's get married this minute. I say to you, "I have married you before God and His Prophet" and you say the same thing to me, then you'll be my wife and I'll be your husband.'

Huda sighs deeply. *So it's to be a marriage of a few moments, an hour, a day or two!*

She hasn't expected her plan to run so smoothly. He sleeps with her, discovers she's a virgin and regrets calling her names and treating her so hatefully, is maybe even sorry that he tried to shut her up, subdue her, sorry for believing that every Muslim woman who didn't cover herself was a fallen woman with no place in society.

'What do you say? Do you accept?'

'Slow down. It must be the Devil tempting you to offer me temporary marriage. You're trying to trick me into thinking that this is a real marriage, even though there are no witnesses and we're not in front of a cleric. All this just so that you can sleep with me.'

'Can we possibly compare the two witnesses, Almighty God and His noble Prophet, peace be upon him, with ordinary human beings?'

'You've convinced me. I accept.'

He quickly turns the key in the lock and hangs a blanket over the metal window blind. The dust from it fills the air. He takes her by the hand and places his other hand on the Quran, saying, 'I have married you before God and His Prophet.'

'I give you myself to enjoy.'

Is this really happening! Huda, the theatre director famous in Toronto for her daring plays, actually speaking these words. She'd always thought this sort of marriage was reserved for the women who used to consult her father: divorcees, old maids, widows, looking for temporary marriages – so-called 'marriages of enjoyment' – in most cases to married men, who didn't want to marry again openly, so married a woman who was like a lover but a lawful lover, halal, permitted by religion. She is like Fadila now, who was addicted to temporary marriages and once asked Huda's father to bless her and agree to absolve her from the statutory waiting period between these marriages, since she would definitely never get pregnant as she was well past fifty.

Hisham jumps. 'Did you say "I give you myself to enjoy"? Are you Shia? Now I understand why you defended Mirza Ghulam.'

'Mirza Ghulam? Who's he?'

'The impostor who claimed that he was the eleventh Imam, the Mahdi, at Speakers' Corner.'

'Ah, that Indian. Yes, my family are Lebanese Shia, and if you want to change your mind because I'm Shia, feel free. I'm used to telling everyone who asks me why I'm not married yet that I'm still waiting for the Mahdi.'

Hisham shakes his head disapprovingly, with a scowl on his face. 'God forbid. That's heresy. I don't understand you at all. I'm sorry to say your ideas are totally unsound.'

'I think it would be better for us both if I left at once.'

'You're right. Goodbye.'

She gets to her feet slowly, half convinced that she is playing with fire, but what's really bothering her is her fear that the strawberry could explode inside her and stain her clothes. How long could that miracle fruit remain in the dark? Would it dissolve automatically if she left it in peace? Would she be able to remove it herself? She tries to calm her nerves. *I could go to a gynaecologist wearing a black abaya and a full-face veil and throw myself on his mercy. 'Oh doctor, I'm not a virgin. I put the strawberry inside me to prove to my bridegroom that I was a virgin when he slept with me for the first time, but he called me a little while ago to say that he wouldn't be arriving until next week.'*

Hisham hurries over to stand by the door, as if to stop her leaving, and says in a low voice, staring at the floor, 'Please don't go. I've fallen in love with you, sister Huda.'

'Can't you stop calling me sister Huda? I don't want to marry my brother.' She bows her head for a moment, then says, 'I have married you before God and His Prophet,' and he quickly places his hand on the Quran, trusting his words will be a waterfall to cool his burning body, and repeats, 'And I have married you before God and His Prophet.'

At this point their bodies are supposed to break free like two horses racing over hills and through fields of sugar cane, but it doesn't happen. He doesn't kiss her or touch her breasts, try to undress her or take his own clothes off. She unzips her jeans and lowers them to mid-thigh, while he flings himself on top of her and begins undoing his flies and taking out his member, then tries to push her knickers to the side and stuff himself into her without success. She congratulates herself. He hasn't disappointed her expectations. As anticipated, he regards her more as a machine than a person. For him she is a body without a head. She helps him, pulling down her knickers with one hand, as if she really is a machine, or like a robot in a women's underwear factory that she'd once seen in a TV programme about Iran. It's just as well, as she wouldn't have been able to face having sex with him if he'd showered her with love and delicate emotions.

As he enters her body, Huda tries to look inside her head. *I don't believe you're having sex with this fanatic,* she says to herself. *All I'm going to think about is the strawberry waiting to explode, and the satisfaction of having my revenge on him when he sees my virginal blood and his arrogance and self-righteousness melt away. His behaviour towards me at Speakers' Corner wasn't that of a believer to a non-believer, but of someone full of contempt and hatred, who wants to impose his ideas on others, and surely that makes him a fanatic.* But as she tries to distract herself in various ways from an overwhelming desire to push Hisham off her, she decides to convince herself that he is forbidden fruit, and this is what will excite her and sustain her enthusiasm. He descends on her as if he is riding an electric bike at speed.

When she tasted the first kiss of her life in Toronto, it occurred to Huda that she might be the only member of her family, indeed the only person in her entire neighbourhood, who had tried kissing. Exchanging kisses seemed like a modern innovation, devised by film directors and people who advocated free love. As an experiment, she brings her lips close to Hisham's and is not surprised when he kisses her without opening his mouth. His lips remain firmly closed like the pockets of a new dress that haven't yet been unstitched. The best kisses were Roberto's. She preferred them even to Mark's. They filled the air with romance. She remembers Roberto and the villa bathed in sun and shadow, while Hisham's prick begins to feel like a hipbone digging into her stomach. It was the surroundings that had made Roberto's kisses so memorable.

She can't help thinking, as she waits for Hisham to get it over with, that this is the first time she has slept with a religious man, and that the men in her family probably have sex with women in this fashion.

Suddenly she pushes him off her. 'Please. Stop, please.' She wriggles uneasily as if she's being throttled and as he lifts himself off her with difficulty she stands up and begins removing her top and jeans and bra. His hands go up to pull hers rapidly out of the way and his pupils move at speed in the whites of his eyes as he attempts to stop her. No, she isn't going to let him do whatever he wants. If she's in this situation, it's because she wants him to face up to his hypocrisy, even without any virginal blood. He wants to have sex with her and go through this fake marriage just to satisfy his desires, but she wants to peel away his groundless religious beliefs like someone peeling an artichoke.

'What's wrong with you? Aren't I your lawful wedded temporary wife? Or do you no longer believe in the marriage vow I repeated before you, with God and His Prophet as witnesses?'

'I don't like the way you're standing there with your chest uncovered. A woman should be modest, even in front of her husband.'

'If you don't want to see me as I am, then you don't really want to get to know me.'

'This body is ephemeral, but the soul is eternal. I'm trying to get to know your soul.'

'Ephemeral! It's in the prime of life!'

He doesn't answer, merely handing her bra and top to her, avoiding looking at her, turning his face to the side. Instead of putting them on, she begins taking off the rest of her clothes, including her knickers. Now she is completely naked. She has escaped again from the burning of the chilli pepper. She wishes she could play the game of the bee and the wasp once more.

'I'm ready,' she calls to Hisham, who puts his hands over his eyes as soon as he sees her naked, as if protecting them from hellfire. In a voice fraught with horror and anger he cries out, 'God forgive me. God protect me from the Devil.' Then he whispers, 'Huda, please. The marriage is invalidated if the husband has sex with his wife when she is naked.'

'Then we won't sleep together.'

She finds herself lying on the bed once more, with him repeating as if he's gone mad, 'I've fallen in love with you, I've fallen in love with you.'

This is the only sentence that has escaped from the nets of religion and fear, and when he begins moving more violently on top of her, Huda's curiosity about the Chinese strawberry increases, as if she's in a chemistry class waiting for the result of an experiment.

He ejaculates over her stomach in silence. At that moment she remembers that she should have screamed like someone experiencing sudden sharp pain, so she screams so loudly that Hisham is afraid a neighbour or a passerby on the pavement outside might hear. Then she begins to wail and cry. How could she produce tears so quickly and spontaneously, as if she really were a virgin? She knows that cunning is the stratagem of the weak, but she isn't weak. She can justify all her actions to herself, and her body is like a plank of wood that has no connection to her thoughts and emotions. That's why she doesn't feel she is betraying Mark.

He gets up off her and makes for the door, to check if anyone has come to see what all the noise is about. It is then that he notices the bright red blood on his member and on the little black hairs that look like a beard with traces of strawberry clinging to it. Again she congratulates herself. She laughs inwardly but modifies the laughter into a faint groan.

'I don't believe it,' he shouts at her. 'Has your indifference towards religion made you so careless in every aspect of your life? Of course you wouldn't know that the true religion forbids a man to approach a woman when she's having her monthly period. Don't you know, you liberated, civilised, modern woman, that having sex with a man during your period exposes both man and woman to all sorts of illnesses? There's a wound there that mustn't be touched until it's completely healed.'

'Can you get me a Kleenex?'

He hurries off to the bathroom, shaking his head in anger and disappointment, and she lifts herself up from the bed. The moment she sees the red stain she smiles to herself. The strawberry has restored her virginity. The red stain spreads joyfully over the bedding. Such a stain has its rites and traditions. If blood flows the girl's family dance in delight and hold their heads high, for it is an irrefutable sign of their daughter's purity, and the bridegroom's family rejoice because he is a true man and has succeeded where others have failed!

She stops herself collapsing into laughter as she remembers the teacher in their 'health education' class saying, 'One drop of blood, yes one drop, travels around a thousand kilometres daily inside a person's body.' And now Huda wants to add, 'Those bloodstains must have travelled millions of kilometres all the way from China before they ended up on this bed.'

When he comes back with some toilet paper and hands it to her, she explodes in his face: 'What's the matter with you religious people! Haven't you heard of virginity, and deflowering virgins?'

He stares at her for a moment, trying to take in what he is hearing, then chews his lip contritely and looks up at the ceiling. 'Thank you, Lord. You are the true benefactor. You guided me to this marriage. I ask Almighty God's forgiveness for every time I have sinned.' His eyes fill with tears. 'I didn't know you were a virgin. You're a true Muslim and I've treated you as if you weren't.'

I see you're all sweetness and light now, you bastard. All this fuss for a few drops of blood, but instead of discussing these things with me this morning, you landed on me like a ton of bricks because I didn't fit into any of your stereotypes.

Aloud she replies both coquettishly and modestly, repeating a phrase she has heard in Arab films, 'This is the wisdom of the Lord.'

A tense silence descends and when he makes no comment, as if he still has doubts about something, she begins to reproach him: 'You were convinced I wasn't a virgin, simply because I didn't wear a headscarf or a face veil. I bet if I was like a sack of coal you wouldn't have got married to me in the way you did.'

'Please don't talk like a Westerner or an Islamophobe about your virtuous covered sisters.'

'You're right, I shouldn't. My name is Huda Kamal from the Bekaa Valley in Lebanon. I work as a teacher in Canada.'

'And I'm Hisham Qasimi. My mother's Egyptian and my father's from Algeria. I study electrical engineering at a college in London as well as working as a doorman in this building.'

As if this reminds him of the blanket stained by the strawberry's virginal blood, he hurries to remove it from the bed.

'I'll throw it in the rubbish bin. I don't want anyone to see it and think bad thoughts about me.'

'Let me wash it for you in the bathroom.'

'No, no, I'll wash it.'

All the same, she folds the blanket so that the red stain isn't visible and hurries to the bathroom where she rubs the spot with soap until it disappears.

'Great.' She's happy with the effect created by the strawberry, and the fact that it hasn't caused any problems and has disappeared without any harmful side effects, leaving Hisham feeling as proud as a peacock and her with a sense of power over him, however slight. Returning to his room, she claps her hands.

'Really great.' She repeats the phrase, anxious to be on her way.

'What do you mean, great? There is nothing great but God. I'll go and get some couscous with chicken from the restaurant, straight after I've prayed.'

I don't want to eat with him! 'The afternoon prayer?'

'No. The prayer for after intercourse. I want to do my ablutions. Please don't open the door to anyone.'

She tries to call Yvonne without success, tidies her hair, powders her forehead and puts on her jacket, all the time trying to pursue the idea of a new play about virginity, a strawberry and a religious man.

He prays clasping his hands to his stomach, like Sunni Muslims do. She doesn't know why they do this differently from Shia. The moment he finishes praying, she says, 'May God accept your prayers,' just as she has heard her parents saying to one another. He remains standing there without moving, looking at her in annoyance.

'What's the matter?'

'To be honest with you, what's bothering me is that you don't behave like a Muslim. For example, you haven't washed after what happened between us, and it's my duty to guide you towards these things.'

Huda never once saw her father trying to communicate with God, instead he used to eat his breakfast at speed, put on his green turban, the colour of Paradise, and sit waiting for people who called him Master so that he could give them guidance. *You're not allowed to guide,* Huda used to think. *'God guides whom He wills.'*

As time passed, she found herself not only welcoming her father's advice and opinions, but also admiring his intelligence and even his ability to dissemble.

People came to him asking him to solve problems relating to religious law and he told them not to bother too much: 'These are trifling matters, that shouldn't concern you,' he would remark. 'Focus on the essence of things in religion.' And they would leave satisfied and content, praising God and thanking Him for His graciousness. Like the woman whose daughters forced her to visit the shaykh when her cursing and swearing got out of hand. He didn't offer her any advice, but fetched a jar of water and put his hand in it, then withdrew it, asking the foul-mouthed woman to do the same. She obeyed in surprise and was on the point of making some vulgar remark, when he forestalled her: 'We've shaken hands now, which means that you've made a pledge not to go back to swearing.' As she said goodbye to Huda's mother, the woman whispered in her ear, 'Poor you. Do the two of you have sex like that in the bathtub?'

'I don't want to wash here,' says Huda to Hisham, smiling coyly.

'It's fine. Go to the bathroom now and say, "There is no god but God" while you wash. Understand?' He hands her a clean, worn towel. She goes into the bathroom, wets the end of the towel with hot water and rubs her stomach, then with her hand she cleans thoroughly between her legs, but doesn't dare to dry herself there in case the red dye stains the towel. She turns the shower full on and under cover of the sound of rushing water she calls Yvonne a few times and when she doesn't get through she leaves a message: 'A girl's honour really can be restored every time, thanks to the strawberry. Ta'abbata Sharran took my virginity, haha. You can't imagine how happy I am. He changed in a flash from a ferocious lion into a peacock strutting around as proud as could be.'

Then she notices a copper jug that must be for ritual ablutions, similar to her father's jug that always used to stand in the corner of their bathroom. She imagines that it's looking at her and begging to be removed from this country. Even though she doesn't go near it, it is asking her, 'Do you remember those days, or have they ceased to have any effect on you, as if they never happened?'

Winking at it, she whispers, 'Mission accomplished,' then looking at herself in the smudged mirror, 'Go on, Huda. Don't stop now.'

When Huda comes out of the bathroom, she finds Hisham completely absorbed in his phone with an expression on his face that she doesn't understand. Then his phone rings and he answers it tersely: 'In a little while. I know. There is no god but God.'

'You haven't washed your hair! What's wrong with you? Why don't you follow religious principles? The hair also has to be purified after sex. "From the top of the head to the tips of the toes!"'

'You're here, not in an Arab country, so you should stop criticising me. I haven't washed my hair because it takes me a lot of time to dry it and style it.'

She plays with her hair and wonders to herself: *Why does religion forbid women to uncover their hair?* She gathers up her hair and ties it back. *What is it about hair that makes it taboo for people to see it? Isn't it just a substance like seaweed or threads on a weaver's loom? A woman's hair is a man's possession: he holds on to it when he's angry, or when he's caressing her.*

'Oh, I understand. Sorry, my bride.' He smiles at her and she realises his smile is him acknowledging that of course she was completely inexperienced until he took her virginity. 'I'm ready to take full responsibility,' he says.

She laughs to herself when he calls her 'my bride', and says he'll take full responsibility. What responsibility? Is he going to marry her for real in a civil ceremony because he's deflowered her? Aren't they supposed to have made love after they were already married with the consent of God and His Prophet? She isn't going to point out his hypocrisy. It's enough that he's almost become a ring on her finger.

She smiles back at him. 'I have to go now. Yvonne's home and she's waiting for me.'

'No, no. Not until we've eaten together. But you never told me how she learnt Arabic.'

'Yvonne's Lebanese like me, even though she's blonde.'

'Her name's Yvonne? I *thought* she wasn't an Arab,' he says in a self-congratulatory tone, as if he's caught a criminal in the act.

'In Lebanon we name people Yvonne and Madeleine, and even Mademoiselle as a first name! She was born with fair hair and green eyes. Everybody thinks she's foreign, and, by the way, I caught you looking at her!'

'It's true, I was keeping an eye on her. I thought she was spying on us, on Muslims, because she looked foreign but she knew Arabic.'

'But you fancied her. I know she's sexy and Arab men love blondes and women with blue or green eyes.'

'I've repented and turned to God. I don't deny that in the past I was totally reckless and frivolous, but I came to my senses, thanks to the will of the Lord. My Lord guided me to the straight path. I used to drink the wine left in customers' glasses when I was working as a waiter. One evening, when I was drinking the dregs from the bottle itself, I heard the call to evening prayer, and it seemed to me that a voice was calling me, reproaching me, so I threw down the bottle and called out, "I repent, Lord" and from that night on I have prayed and fasted and read the holy books.'

'Where did that happen? In Algeria?'

'In London! It was a recording on the cell phone of a man from the Gulf who mistook the kitchen for the gents'. Will you tell her about what's happened between us?'

'No, no. She's Christian and she'd think that what you and I agreed on was a kind of madness.'

'On the contrary, she'll envy you because Islam is a flexible religion as regards marriage and divorce. Why should your friend's reaction be one of disapproval? Didn't my marriage to you guarantee your honour and self-respect? I respected both your body and your soul and didn't treat you like soiled goods.'

'If I'd been soiled goods, I wouldn't have been a virgin!'

'Why were you still a virgin? Of course, it was because in all these years you'd never found a man who was a sincere believer, the sort your parents advised you to marry. Rest assured, I'm ready to take all the responsibility.'

Ah, Arab chivalry, she laughs to herself, then aloud, 'Perhaps I should go now.'

'But we agreed to eat together. Shall we go and get something in Golborne Road? It's not far from here.'

Have you lost your mind? Do you think I'd go anywhere with you?

But she agrees in the end. The image of him muttering 'In the Name of God the Compassionate, the Merciful' comes to her mind and takes her back to a language she's pretended to forget at various stages of her life. Just the sight of the bobbles on his socks, because they've been washed so often with other clothes, reminds her of her father's and brother's socks and evokes warm feelings in her.

Huda walks along with Hisham. They go down quiet streets, past houses and cafés, crossing a bridge where the cars rush by so fast that Huda is almost knocked over in the slipstream.

They are going along Oxford Street, which is thronged with dozens of tourist rickshaws and echoes to the sound of Arab songs, acting like magnets to draw in the Arabs walking by. Sports cars roar and growl, their Arab drivers competing to see who can make the loudest noise.

Vagrants and beggars, Roma, Europeans begging from Arabs in broken Arabic and using incorrect quotes from the Quran, phrases used to praise and thank God, rather than to ask for alms, that they must have got from translation sites on the internet. Women swathed in black abayas fly along in the rickshaws like a flock of black doves singing songs of thwarted love, but laughing and happy to be in the heart of London.

I'm going to be a tourist in London with Mark. She found herself texting him, asking him to wish her luck for tomorrow's meeting at the theatre.

A pretty young blonde woman is begging, her head bent close to the ground, looking as if she's acting a part, raising her bowed head from time to time, and in her hands is a sheet of paper with Arabic writing on it, obviously handwritten by an Arab: 'As for the poor, do not rebuff them. The Almighty has spoken the truth.'

'With Almighty God's help the Arabic language will become as important as English,' Hisham says, looking at the beggar.

'And the shisha will take the place of beer!' responds Huda.

When Hisham gives her a disapproving look, she thinks, *Why am I with this guy, why don't I tell him to fuck off and be on my way?*

They board a bus taking them to Ladbroke Grove.

She breathes a sigh of relief when she sees that his attention is focused entirely on his phone, as if it's his hand or a third eye. He never stopped consulting it when they were in his room, even after they'd had sex, as if he was confiding his impressions to the machine and it was agreeing or disagreeing.

'I'm trying to find a shop whose owner I used to know. I want to buy something, something for you!'

He wants to buy me a wedding ring. It's time to leave. But I can trick him, vanish like a mustard seed in a forest, she tells herself comfortingly.

'Oh, thanks, I don't want anything.'

She notices that they're walking along Golborne Road and that it's not how she expected. She'd read that it was like a microcosm of the Maghreb, an area known as 'Little Morocco', but it is groaning with loneliness, the tables of its restaurants and cafés almost deserted, a mosque with bearded men at its door, a Portuguese patisserie. One of the cafés reminds her of a café in Beirut frequented by men only, who spent their whole time playing backgammon. Men from the Maghreb smoke cigarettes and shishas inside and outside. Hisham stops suddenly to talk to a shopkeeper and Huda can barely make out what the two men are saying even though they're talking Arabic.

On display here are caftans, kitchen utensils, and ceramic and earthenware vessels, including Moroccan tagines. She breathes a sigh of relief as she realises that Hisham isn't thinking of buying her a wedding ring. Strange, the word used for a wedding ring in Arabic: *mahbis,* also meaning prison.

Hisham fingers the shawls hanging at the shop's entrance and asks Huda to choose one. She declines as she never wears such things, and besides, these are particularly ugly and made of cheap polyester and scratchy nylon. As they move to another rack, she glances at their reflection in the shop's mirror and sees someone who must surely be her double at Ta'abbata Sharran's side. She feels immense regret that she has agreed to eat with him, that what she did with him in his room somehow indicates that they're in cahoots, co-conspirators.

'You really don't have to buy me anything.'

What she wants most of all is to get rid of this mill-stone round her neck, i.e., Hisham, but she's promised to have dinner with him, so that's what she'll do. In any case, she's hungry. She just has to put up with his company for another hour or two, then today will become no more than a strange memory. On this occasion, she doesn't proclaim her opinion out loud, although it's not like her to hold back from saying when something upsets her. He insists, pleads with her: 'Please, we're going to a restaurant belonging to a friend of mine and I want you to agree to cover your head,' and he hands her a dark brown shawl.

'Let's go to another restaurant, then.'

'Please. Please, Huda.'

'Hisham, for goodness' sake, look at the tight jeans I'm wearing, this fitted top. I don't want anyone to see me with a hijab. "The neck upwards belongs to God. What's below the neck belongs to man." I don't want to have that saying quoted at me.'

'That's disgusting. Shame on you.'

She leaves the shop, pleased with her excuse, but he hurries after her, still carrying the shawl and apologising to her in a way that makes her think, *I'm crazy. I deserve everything that's happening to me. 'If you play with a cat, expect to get scratched', as they say.*

She goes back into the shop with him and changes the brown shawl for another, more colourful, and arranges it on her head before the shop's smudged mirror, at which point Hisham suddenly descends on her with expressions of admiration, sounding to her astonishment as if he is being flirtatious: 'Praise God! Your face is as radiant as the sun or the moon. I don't know what to say!'

These compliments make her recoil like a snail sprinkled with salt. She is filled with remorse: he's sincere and she's a hypocrite and a liar. But isn't he the one who has indirectly forced her to become a hypocrite, so that she can get even with him? Then another flattering remark from him makes her start spinning her web again, like a spider whose eyes have suddenly come back into focus.

'That pretty face of yours would be even prettier if you wore a veil.'

He sees her expression, which says plainly, 'Have you gone mad?'

'Why are you scared? I didn't say a niqab, just a piece of transparent material over your face, and it won't hinder your movements in any way, trust me.'

'You must be joking! It's crazy. Your eyes should be visible, and then your heart and mind are visible too. But tell me, what's the point of covering my face if people can still see my features?'

'The point is that it makes the woman's face as a whole less provocative. The niqab only reveals the eyes, where the greatest provocation resides. What we're talking about is the provocation that is more powerful than death, the provocation of a woman's beauty. Don't we describe a woman as alluring, or enticingly beautiful? As the saying goes, "Ask God's protection from being led astray by beauty."'

'But why are you scared of beauty instead of thanking God for it?'

'Anyway, please cover your head with the shawl in the restaurant, for my sake.'

If only their conversation could have carried on in this vein so she could have walked away and left Hisham alone with his thoughts, instead of discovering that she was both fish and bait, for as soon as she enters the restaurant to keep him happy, two bearded men rise to welcome him from a table where two women and a couple of small children are talking noisily. One of the women wears a hijab and the other a niqab. Hisham greets them with an abrupt 'Peace be upon you'.

Huda smiles at the two women. The one in the hijab smiles back, while the one wearing the niqab, who is enveloped in black from head to foot, contents herself with a welcoming nod of the head. The two men, the husbands of these women, appear to have decided rapidly that Huda doesn't exist. She sits down on the vacant chair next to the woman in a hijab, who has a nice face.

'Hallo, sister.'

'Hallo. My name's Huda.'

'Pleased to meet you, Huda. My name's Suad.'

The woman with the faceless head says, 'What a beautiful name, Huda, the light of God's guidance. I'm your sister, Aisha.'

The restaurant is packed with Arabs: families with children, young girls probably no more than nine years old with their heads covered, running and playing and laughing as if their headscarves came into being at the same time as their hair and don't stop them playing and causing havoc like other children. Young men with the latest haircuts and clothes sit around a table laughing noisily to the accompaniment of songs that are a mixture of Eastern and Western. Suddenly the woman called Aisha protests: 'No! Not Sami Yusuf again. We're fed up with hearing him.'

'Who's Sami Yusuf?' asks Huda, raising her voice to attract Hisham's attention so she can urge him to move to a table where they can be on their own, get their food quickly and leave. Or maybe it's better if she just leaves once and for all.

But Suad, who has an Egyptian accent, hurries to answer Huda's question with real enthusiasm: 'I can't believe you've never heard of Sami Yusuf. Where have you been living?'

'In Canada.'

'Ah, I understand. You've got a good excuse.'

Huda listens to the song and as it booms out again Aisha gets to her feet in protest, only to be restrained by her bearded husband, demanding that she sit down: 'Whatever's wrong with you?'

My best times were when I felt close to you
But everything fell apart the moment I strayed from you
In each smile, in every sigh, every minute detail
Traces of you are found there
Wherever you are, I'll find you 'cause you're the one I turn to
Wherever you are, I'll be with you
'Cause you're the one my heart belongs to.
I need you.

Huda looks at Aisha and nods her head as if agreeing with her, for the song is naïve and sentimental. All the same, it ignites the enthusiasm of the majority of customers and especially the young men with the latest haircuts, who stand up around their table, close their eyes and raise their arms in supplication as if performing a piece of theatre. When the song is almost over they prostrate themselves humbly and the whole restaurant applauds. The song is a Sufi prayer addressed to God, not to a human lover.

Next comes a song by Yusuf Islam, formerly known as Cat Stevens, called 'A Is for Allah', followed by Doris Day singing 'Que sera, sera'. Amazed as Huda is to hear the song in these surroundings, she listens to it differently this time round and can believe that Doris Day is singing to God, the only one who knows and understands the secrets that the future holds.

Whatever will be, will be
The future's not ours to see

Dishes of couscous, vegetables and chicken arrive at the table.

'Can we eat now?' Huda asks Hisham, having tried without success to catch his eye. He's either avoiding looking at her, or he's completely ruled by his two bearded friends, especially the one who never raises his eyes from his prayer beads, indifferent to his wife Suad. She, meanwhile, is busy with the toddler in her lap and a little girl, presumably her daughter, who looks about five.

When Hisham doesn't show any sign of answering her question, Aisha the faceless says, 'You're welcome, sister. With pleasure. Of course, please help yourself.' Everyone excuses themselves and goes to wash their hands, returning to sit at the table and say 'In the Name of God the Compassionate the Merciful' before they start eating, just as she used to do in her parents' house when they taught her to thank God for this blessing.

As she reaches for the food, Hisham stops her, not because she hasn't said 'In the Name of God' but because she hasn't washed her hands as she is supposed to do before eating. She suppresses her anger and embarrassment in front of the others, who pretend not to notice what Hisham has done, but is exasperated by the fact that he feels at liberty to reprimand her. 'Oh sorry, I forgot.' She goes out to the bathroom, wishing the restaurant had another door so she could escape. To spite him, she doesn't wash her hands and comes back pretending to shake the water off them. As she reaches for the food once more, he hands her some dried figs: 'It's better for you to begin your meal with figs so the stomach is ready to digest vegetables and meat, as it instructs us in the Quran.'

She is hungry. The delicious food descends her gullet: grains of couscous and morsels of fragrant chicken transport her right back to reality.

She can't help staring at Aisha as she pushes the food into her mouth under the black niqab. She's like a hooded falcon. When the falcon's hood is removed, it spreads its wings and flies up into the air, but she wonders what Aisha does when they remove the niqab from her face. Does she fly like a bird? This image gleams in her imagination and she thinks of using it in the British version of *One Thousand and One Nights.*

Huda notices the bearded man, Suad's husband, speaking in whispers with Hisham, his frown deepening, while the other bearded man, Aisha's husband, merely nods or shakes his head. Then the three men suddenly move on to another table.

Now I've eaten, I have to leave, thinks Huda. But a woman from another table seizes the opportunity of the men's absence and descends on Suad, whispering something in her ear. Suad says disparagingly out loud, 'You're right, my bag is Christian Dior, but it's a copy, a fake!'

Suad turns her back on the woman, ignoring her and reaching out a hand to Huda's earring, as if deliberately taking a different tack, to prompt the woman to leave. 'Your earrings are really unusual. They're beautiful. Did you buy them here?'

'I inherited them from my grandmother. They're Ottoman half-lira coins.'

But Suad ceases to be interested in Huda's earrings, because she is distracted by the woman saying as she leaves, 'OK fine, there is no god but God,' and Suad and Aisha reply, 'And Muhammad is His Prophet.' Then at once Suad begins telling Huda and Aisha how the woman came to ask her to boycott Christian Dior products on account of his name. Huda and Aisha laugh. 'I don't believe it!' remarks Huda, while Aisha says, 'It's not relevant whether the bag's a copy or an original. You should have just told her that we Muslims believe in Jesus Christ too.'

'You're right. It's a waste of time talking to her. I don't like that woman. She's trying to set herself up as our leader. She's contacted me hundreds of times asking me to sign a petition in protest against the Egyptian shaykh who's issued a fatwa making it legal for a husband to eat his wife in times of famine. I told her this was rubbish and we'd do better to ignore him.'

Huda has clearly taken to Suad and she begins to joke with her. 'OK, let's tell her the man's wife would be starving too if there was a severe famine, so she'd be nothing but skin and bone!'

Suad laughs. She's probably in her twenties and her kohl-rimmed eyes laugh with her, beneath eyebrows like two swords.

Once more Sami Yusuf's singing fills the restaurant, and once more Aisha objects: 'Why doesn't everyone understand that there's nothing special about Sami Yusuf even if he does sing mainly religious songs?'

'But he attracts young men to religion with his songs, and that's important! His music attracts them more effectively than fatwas issued by shaykhs or incitements to kill for a cause, or for no cause at all,' says Suad.

'Yes, and he attracts females too. His photos are just like those of any other star, focusing on his face and hair and lips ...'

'No, you're wrong there, my dear Aisha!' says Suad.

'Listen, now that you and I and Huda are all firm friends, I have to tell you that I think you're physically attracted to Sami Yusuf. I'm afraid for you. Your love for him, even though it's at a distance, is a kind of adultery and you're a wife and mother.'

Suad changes the subject and praises Huda's beauty, thanking God who has blessed Hisham with the chance to meet her. 'Praise the Lord who brought you from Canada to London so he could get to know you.'

At this point, instead of telling them she'd only met Hisham that day and only known him for a few hours, so few that they could be counted on the fingers of one hand, she leans forward to embrace Suad and kiss Aisha on the shoulder, apologising that it's time for her to leave.

'No, don't be angry, darling,' cries Suad. 'Hisham had to go off with our husbands because they didn't want to stay with us after your shawl fell down on to your shoulders. Mind you, they only mentioned that once they'd stuffed themselves with food. Such hypocrisy! In any case, the second witness is running late and should show up at any moment. By the way, Hisham is a good man – he didn't signal to you to cover your hair. My husband sometimes tries to get me to cover myself even when we're alone together. The marriage ceremony won't take more than five or ten minutes, but while it's going on you'll absolutely have to keep the shawl on your head. I wish,' continues Suad, 'that women could be official witnesses at a marriage ceremony, then Aisha and I could have been your witnesses. I really like you.'

Huda's heart sinks and she suddenly feels dizzy. She gulps, her mouth dry. She must escape this minute – outwit him and get away.

'Would you believe me if I told you that this is the first I've heard of this marriage?'

'Maybe Hisham wanted to surprise you!'

'No, listen to me, I didn't know him before. I met him a few hours ago. And what happened, happened.'

Then, annoyed at herself for being so demure in front of the women, even though it was for their own sake, she says boldly, no longer holding back, 'I agreed to have sex with him after he'd insisted that we had to say to one another, "I have married you before God and His Prophet".'

'And did you both sign something?' says Suad quickly.

'No. Anyhow, thanks so much, and goodbye.'

'Hang on, darling. You're absolutely right. Hisham should have told you that he wanted to formalise the marriage in front of two witnesses in order to clear his conscience; it won't do; he's treated you unfairly, but his intentions are pure.'

'Never mind about Hisham,' intervenes Aisha. 'Think about the Almighty and how pleased He'll be with you, how He'll forgive this sin of yours.'

'Thanks for everything. But it's really time for me to go.' Now Huda doesn't pause, even when Suad stands up to say goodbye to her, or conceivably to ask her to stay a bit longer. Huda plunges out of the restaurant like a wild horse, Hisham hurrying after her, apologising for having left her with the two women.

'Not at all. It's the best thing that could have happened to me. You're the biggest liar I've ever met. You've been plotting and scheming behind my back. Now I realise why you wanted me to wash my hair, so that you could arrange this marriage with your stupid friends. But at least you left me with two truthful women. Go on, get back to the restaurant. The witness must be on his way.'

'Please Huda, please, I'm sorry. If I didn't tell you before, it was because I didn't want to make you worried, and because I was afraid you'd think it was a complicated process, whereas in fact it couldn't be simpler! Somebody recites the Fatiha before two witnesses and we repeat it after them, just like that, in a family gathering in the restaurant, no mosque or officiating clergy.'

'Why didn't you think about that when we were in your room? You should have explained to me before we slept together that having Almighty God and His Prophet, peace be upon him, as witnesses wasn't sufficient. If I'd known that we'd also need two human beings as witnesses, I'd have refused for sure.'

'I changed my mind because I didn't know before that you were a virgin. When I discovered that you'd preserved your virginity up till then, I was sure you'd held fast to your religion without being conscious of it.'

Come on, Huda, tell him the whole story, starting with the game of the bee and the wasp and ending with the virginity strawberry, the proof of it still on the bathroom window ledge.

'Please, Huda, forgive me and agree to have the Fatiha recited in front of two witnesses. That's all I ask of you.'

Maybe you're tricking me into marrying you for real, because you've fallen in love with me.

But aloud she says to him: 'Marry in front of two witnesses to confirm that we aren't hypocrites and are being honest to God and to ourselves? Sorry, I'll never ever agree to that.'

'Even if I were to tell you that I'm asking the Lord to pardon me for being driven by my animal instincts? I know I won't be able to sleep a wink until I marry before two witnesses.'

'But, let me say again, we've married and fulfilled all the requirements in front of two excellent witnesses without violating any laws, so I don't understand why we should call two human beings to witness our marriage. What's happened has happened, and I don't think we'll be sleeping together again. In any case, I live in Canada and I'll be leaving in a few days and never coming back. That's the reality. Canada's where I work and where my life is.'

'I know that. I'm not asking you to change anything. All that concerns me is that you help me return to the straight path. Every marriage should take place in front of witnesses, even a temporary marriage like ours. There are those who say that a marriage can be valid without witnesses in rare cases when it's impossible to find any, and then the couple marries as we have already done. But I ought to have got hold of two witnesses. We're not living in the jungle.'

'Sorry, you should have left me in your room and rushed out into the street and fetched two witnesses, or else opened the window instead of putting a blanket over it, and shouted, "Good people, I need two witnesses straight away."'

'That's enough, please. I don't want to compound my sins. I've done wrong and I don't want what happened between us to look like prostitution or sex outside marriage.'

'Prostitution? So that was prostitution for free, since I didn't take a penny from you! Sorry, apart from the couscous.'

'Please stop talking like this, or else …' He looms in front of her, eyes bulging, as if he's about to hit her.

'Or else what?' she replies loudly, summoning what courage she can. 'You want to put into practice what you said this morning at Speakers' Corner? "The hen must be slaughtered when she cries louder than the rooster."'

'I'm sorry for that. But listen to me, I confess I've made a nonsense of religion and moved away from God and His Prophet and God's anger has descended upon me.'

What actually descends on him at the door of the restaurant is the hand of the second witness, who begins apologising for being late. When he greets Huda, smiling, she immediately remembers seeing him in Hyde Park that morning, joking with the African monk. Clearly worried that the witness will notice him pleading with Huda, Hisham says quickly, 'Everyone's waiting for you inside. We'll join you in a few moments.'

Huda hails a taxi but Hisham rushes to prevent her opening the door, catching hold of her hand and saying to the driver, 'Sorry, we have some urgent business to finish.'

'Good luck with that,' says the driver sarcastically and speeds off.

'Huda, please, you must help me. Ten minutes, no more. Remember how I helped you when you weren't feeling well, put my job at risk by taking you to the place where I work. Remember it was you who seduced me; you put your arms round me first and you didn't object to anything I did. Forgive me for mentioning it, but remember how you undressed in front of me! Now we have to marry in front of two witnesses, and maybe you're pregnant by me, for virgins can get pregnant even from the smell of a man. That's all I have to say. The rest is up to you and your conscience.'

Huda bows her head as if hoping the ground at her feet will open and swallow her up, but the lights of an approaching taxi beckon to her and like magic she's on board, then in a flash Hisham enters by the opposite door and sits next to her, an octopus clinging to its prey.

Should she tell the driver she doesn't know this man so he'll stop the car and throw him out? But Hisham is acting like a relative, a friend, a brother. She gives the driver an address before retreating into silence, instinctively aware that Hisham is insisting on accompanying her to find out where she is staying with Yvonne. The taxi stops at the address she has given to the driver, that of Yvonne's office. They get out and she pays the fare. She enters the code at high speed so that Hisham can't learn it, hears the buzz and pushes the door open.

She goes in, waving goodbye to him, takes the lift to the top floor then descends the stairs to the ground floor. She calls Yvonne again but doesn't get through: her friend must be submerged in the noise of the wedding. She opens the door and looks up and down the street to make sure that Hisham has really gone, then hails a taxi and gives the driver Yvonne's home address. She clasps her hands together, trying to calm herself down in a voice that all of London can hear.

Yvonne looks down at her dress constantly as she drives to St Ethelburga's Church in the City of London to attend the wedding reception of a neighbour who is now a close friend, though he never became a lover. Was she wrong to wear the yellow dress instead of the turquoise one that Huda favoured?

Today Yvonne, by choosing the colour yellow, seems to want to tell herself and everyone there that she is like a daffodil opening in the warmth of the sun.

She parks her car ten minutes away from the church. The narrow passageway leading to the chapel is not really what she is expecting, but it opens out into a courtyard and garden behind the church, with guests everywhere. So this is where she is going to hunt for a man – no, not hunt, for the prey is never happy when it falls into the hunter's hands. She will ensnare a man in this perfect setting. She has tried before on every possible occasion: funerals, doctors' waiting rooms, social gatherings, at the supermarket, even in the underground when she started using it from time to time instead of driving her car; not to mention the countless clubs, gyms and dance classes she joined.

Yvonne pretends to be interested in everything she sees in the church garden except the men. She inspects the plants and even stops in front of a statue that doesn't interest her at all, noticing out of the corner of her eye that the women are looking at her dress. She feels reassured, its beauty has become almost like protective armour, giving her confidence. She smiles and talks to people, telling some of them that she is divorced, her eyes following the men, transformed into instruments for distinguishing between the single, the married, and the gay. She bends down and picks up a little girl, and spins her around like a top, trying to make her laugh to attract people's attention, as she has learnt from her mistakes that she should appear natural and happy even if she doesn't have a man or a child. Gone are the days when she used to exchange emails with her friends and with women she didn't know about the long wait for a boyfriend, feeling glad when someone wrote: 'Don't despair! Who knows? Lightning may be about to strike!'

She put those days behind her when she found herself with other women at a birthday party that changed suddenly from a joyous occasion into a kind of wake, all of them lamenting their bad luck and tears flowing freely, especially when someone played a Connie Francis song from the sixties: '*Where the boys are, someone waits for me, A smiling face, a warm embrace, Two arms to hold me tenderly.*' Then someone else remarked, 'Do you want to know how they thought of adding salt to chocolate? It was my tears falling on it.'

There was even a professional biologist in this circle of disappointed women, who tried to revive their hopes by explaining to them that love was like bacteria, both useful and harmful. Of course bacteria helped ferment cheese, turn milk into yoghurt and pump plants with vitamins, but at the same time they could be deadly to humans, plants and animals. Yes, love devours people like a swarm of gnats.

Yvonne gives the little girl back to her mother and moves on to talk to an elderly man, trying to make him feel as if he were young again, smiling at him, her eyes shining. She hurries over to kiss the bride, who retreats and blows Yvonne a kiss, whispering, 'I'm afraid for my make-up.'

'Then I'll give Ghulam two kisses.'

The old Yvonne would have answered, 'Come on, why do you care about your make-up? You've caught a man and now you're a bride.'

A couple hurry in with their child, heaving sighs of relief because the wedding festivities haven't begun yet, telling the bride and groom that their train stopped four stations away and they had to take the bus.

I ought to be grateful that I've been so lucky in my life. It's better to have a car than a kid you have to drag around on public transport. But she immediately rebukes herself for having such thoughts: *Don't forget, you never went in a car until you were twelve years old!*

She removes her shoes before entering the tent that they called 'The Tent of all Faiths'. The word 'Peace' is written over the tent door in different languages: English, Arabic, Hebrew, Hindi, accompanied by the symbols of different religions. She stacks her shoes with the others outside the tent, as requested on the invitation, pleased to see that hers are more striking than all the rest. She had spent about an hour, with Huda's help, choosing shoes and tights that people would notice.

'Cinderella's shoes!' exclaimed Huda, seizing hold of them. Yvonne had bought them in China. They were made of grass-green silk, with plants and fishes embroidered on them in orange thread. 'Yvonne, everyone who sees them will rush to find out who they belong to.'

Yvonne sits down in the big camel-hair tent that was said to be an authentic Bedouin tent. But here there is no tribal shaykh with his guests in their Bedouin clothes, as they appeared in school textbooks, with someone pounding coffee beans nearby, the regular sound in the stillness of the desert night gladdening the hearts of caravans of travellers guided by its rhythm to the tent. Instead the members of the tribe in this tent are engaged in battles with their children, who refuse to stop rolling around on the Persian rugs and jumping on the cushions and ottomans, their fair heads and dark heads bobbing up and down as they reach up to touch the sun and moon in the stained-glass windows.

When relative calm eventually prevails in the tent, the din grows louder in Yvonne's head: *Why didn't any of the Lebanese who were against the sectarian war think of erecting a tent like this to call for peace and dialogue and understanding between those inflexible minds, instead of fleeing to another country or hiding away in the air-raid shelters like rats!* Then rejecting her own question: *A tent of peace in the midst of war. The shells would have pulverised it within seconds, those involved in its construction would be dead and fire would have consumed all the expressions of peace and love over its entrance. And now Lebanon's back in the headlines because of what's happening in Syria: ISIS, refugees, Hizbullah, Iran.*

The bride's aunt, sitting on Yvonne's right, seems to guess what Yvonne is thinking. She asks whether she's a friend of the bride or the groom. When Yvonne introduces herself, the aunt asks if she is one hundred per cent Lebanese, as she looks European.

'Do you visit Lebanon?'

'Yes, every year or two.'

'But the situation there … ?'

'The situation there sickens me. Religions flourish and catch fire and devour people once they're nicely roasted,' answers Yvonne, her irritable tone unsuited to the festive occasion and the atmosphere of tranquillity in the tent.

Somewhat disconcerted, the aunt remarks, 'Ah, religions. But don't you agree with me that it's a wonderful idea for Sophie and Ghulam to get married in this tent?'

'Absolutely,' answers Yvonne, smiling, even though her Adam's apple is about to explode from the confusion that has recently resurfaced in her. *Am I still Lebanese? Shall I turn the page of Lebanon and my family? Perhaps I've half turned it already. If I'd stayed in Lebanon, I wouldn't be on my own now, I'd have got married and my family would have stuffed me with food like the white goose so that my bridegroom the ghoul could devour me.*

In her childhood Yvonne used to hear the story of the ghoul who kidnapped a young girl and began bringing her food and more food. One day she said to the ghoul, 'Oh Ghoul, you're the opposite of what I've heard about you, for you feed me instead of eating me. In fact you give me more food than my family does.' The ghoul answered, 'Of course. I'm feeding you to fatten you up and then I'll enjoy eating you, for now you are skinny and I'm worried I might crack my teeth on your bones.'

The smell of sweaty feet rises into her nostrils. When she asked her mother to buy her a pair of slippers with Mickey Mouse's face on them, like the ones owned by the girl next door, her mother instead brought out her big brother Tanius's old tennis shoes. She grabbed hold of a sharp knife to cut them down to size, having failed with the big kitchen scissors, then stuffed Yvonne's feet into them, indifferent to her shouting and wailing. 'No, Mum. These aren't slippers and they're too big for my feet. No, no, they stink, Mum, they stink. They smell like mothballs. Please, Mum.'

A tall young man with brown hair and blue eyes comes into the tent and appears undecided whether to sit in the front row or the second row where she is sitting. She rejoices inwardly when he sits down next to her. *Thank God I didn't stay in Lebanon. I'm a citizen of the world.* The young man turns to her. 'My legs are so long they'll get in the way if I sit in the front row,' indicating the seat in front of him. Is he apologising because he doesn't want her to feel flattered that he has chosen to sit next to her! To herself she says, *Thank God your legs are long. I've always liked praying mantises and tried to pick them up, and your legs remind me of theirs.*

The bride and groom enter, followed by a man wearing no clerical garb of any sort, a doctor of theology according to the order of service. He begins by reciting some verses from the Quran in a disagreeable Arabic accent, repeating several times the word *'Neeka, Nika'* which Yvonne doesn't understand. Is it a foreign word? It sounds like an Arabic word for having sex, but a vulgar swear word. She remembers something the witty Tahir said at Speakers' Corner about the ban on Nike sports shoes. Yvonne looks around the audience and when she doesn't see any of Ghulam's Iranian relatives smiling or looking disapproving, she begins reading the service sheet and quickly finds the word *nikah*. She never knew before that it was also a synonym for the word for marriage and was used with that meaning in the Quran and the official Muslim marriage ceremony.

The word *nikah* is a thread in the spider's web that she is spinning to catch the praying mantis. She acts as if she is fighting an overwhelming desire to laugh, covering her mouth with one hand and eyes with the other, but soon she is shaking with laughter, although she carries on pretending that she is trying in vain to suppress it. Praying

Mantis nudges her and whispers, 'What's so funny?' and she whispers back, 'He's repeating an old word that must be a synonym for the usual word for marriage.'

'What is it?'

'*Nikah*. It means sex, screwing, fucking.'

'But how do you know Persian?'

'It's an Arabic word. He's reading from the Quran.'

'Have you studied Arabic?'

'I'm Lebanese.'

'*Neeka, neeka.*'

She spins another thread. '*Nikah.*'

'*Nikakh.*'

She brings her mouth close to his ear and repeats '*Nikah-h-h-h*', making the 'h' like the hissing of a snake.

'Shhhh.' Somebody tries to shut her up.

She can't believe her luck. A totally attractive man of around her own age, sitting next to her and asking her questions about the word for having sex. He's probably already had an image of the two of them together on a bed, or doing it standing up. She stops herself getting carried away by her yearnings. Perhaps he is just asking. Perhaps his curiosity to know about different languages, multiculturalism, is making him ask, not his desire for her. She regrets using the words screwing and fucking. Maybe making love would have sounded more feminine.

She no longer allows her fantasies to play tricks on her. She's tired of analysing and interpreting and feels like Eliza Doolittle: 'Don't talk of stars, burning above, If you're in love, show me!' *Did a man behave like that to me because he ... ? Did he mean something else? Was he too shy to hold my hand, or was he disgusted by that single black hair on my chin that I forgot to pluck?* She went so far as to imagine that men ran away from her because they were afraid she would put their manhood under a microscope and they wouldn't be able to fulfil her desires, or she would take over their lives and their personalities would dissolve into nothing.

A golden shaft of sunlight enters the tent and there is complete calm. The monotony of the marriage ceremony is sending the children to sleep. Yvonne is in a warm bubble, far removed from her surroundings. She feels happy and confident, the energy flooding back into her life. This change isn't thanks to the hours she has spent with an analyst, following Huda's repeated advice to her over the months, when she was still pouring out her suffering on to the pages of the internet, and in repeated calls to Huda across the Atlantic. She has lost weight. Her thighs, arms, stomach and waist have shrunk, as if the kilos have flown away into the air. Her eyes are larger, her neck longer, she looks taller.

She sinks down among the cushions. The bride and groom are still listening to the man performing the ceremony, as if they are students and he is their teacher. She wonders if they are really listening to what he is saying. The guests follow intently a service that is religious and not religious at the same time, and now he is talking about the bonds of affection that will never alter or change as long as they live.

She studies her neighbour's long legs and gives a shudder of fear, not because he is the giant in 'Jack and the Beanstalk', but because she is becoming eccentric. All she yearns for now is his legs. *That's enough. Please don't play these games with me,* she counsels herself. *We've turned a page and today is the beginning of a new era. You want this praying mantis, not just his legs.* She defends herself: *His legs are what I like. I want to sit with his legs, embrace them, talk to them. I'll ask him excitedly, 'Can I see your legs this evening? Are they free? Please ask them when and where. Tell me where they are taking you and I'll hurry to meet them.'*

The guests applaud and Ghulam bends to kiss Sophie after they have crammed wedding rings on each other's fingers. Trills of joy rise from Iranian throats, while an elderly Englishman comments to his wife, 'This is a strange wedding. I didn't understand what the man said when he conducted the Muslim part of the ceremony. Is it to our darling Sophie's advantage or not? She'd better be careful.'

Yvonne leaves the tent with the others, dawdling to fasten her Chinese shoes. She looks around for Praying Mantis but just when she is beginning to despair, she hears his voice: 'Ha! So you're the owner of those amazing shoes. The only ones without heels. Where did you get them?'

'From Shanghai.'

'Do they speak Arabic there?'

'Of course.'

He looks at her as if to say, 'You're good fun. You look as if nothing bothers you.'

They walk together into the courtyard where the newly-weds stand receiving congratulations. Praying Mantis stops to talk to someone. She doesn't stand beside him as she would have done before, but keeps going, smiling and greeting people she knows and some she doesn't, circulating until she finds out his name: James F. She looks for the room where the reception will shortly be held, then searches through the guest list pinned to the door for their names and table numbers. The room is still empty except for a few waiters and she exchanges a card with an Iranian name on it in the place to the right of hers with that of James F. She feels a pang of remorse but remembers the old saying 'Luck helps those that help themselves.'

She congratulates the couple before going to sign the big card, but wants to draw them, rather than write a message as most are doing. She makes it so the bridal veil takes up the whole length of the card and decorates it with little birds and flowers and butterflies and rainbows and her signature is the wing of one of the butterflies. She would go to huge lengths to make sure that James sees what she has drawn. The days are gone when she tried to attract men by giving them shirts and ties and embroidered robes.

She goes over to settle into the seat beside Praying Mantis.

'Cinderella Yvonne!' he shouts. 'I don't believe it. We sat together in the tent and we're sitting together at the reception!'

'I worked miracles to get to sit next to you. I changed the place arrangement.'

'Yeah, yeah, I believe you!' He'd have been just as sceptical if she'd told him that she had imagined herself as his bride when they were in the tent. Techno music rings out.

'Did you write anything on the card? The groom's mother saw me drawing the couple and insisted that I make Ghulam taller, so I did, but she still wanted me to give him a few extra centimetres, and when I explained that it would be difficult to do for technical reasons, she suggested that I make the bride shorter than she really is!'

James laughs and leaves the table suddenly without apologising or giving a reason. She thanks God they are sitting at a table, otherwise he would have claimed he was going to get a refill, then not come back.

He returns with a delighted expression on his face. 'Ha! Ghulam looks like a giant next to Sophie. I love the drawing. Are you an artist?'

'I work in advertising,' she says, taking it as a good sign that her drawing had caught his attention. That must mean he was attracted to her. 'When I said to his mother that Ghulam looked much taller than Sophie, even though Sophie was actually taller than him, she replied that Ghulam was taller than he looked, but the way he carried himself made him look shorter, and of course Sophie wasn't short!'

'Does your mother think you're taller than you really are?' laughs James.

'When I was sixteen I asked her to buy me a pair of high heels and she answered sarcastically that I should remain as I was, then if I dropped an egg it wouldn't break.' James interrupts her with a laugh but she continues, 'So what could I do but take an egg from the fridge and drop it on the tiled floor of the living room.'

She doesn't disclose to him what her mother said after she hit her: 'You're more trouble than you're worth.' Nor how her mother had made her spoon up the yolk and the white that looked like vomit, then fried it and tried to force Yvonne to eat it, until her father arrived and saved her.

'You should thank your mother. Women who wear heels walk like giraffes with backache, whereas your wonderful shoes make you look graceful. Do you think Cinderella was graceful?'

'Of course! But would you like to take my shoes and give them to your girlfriend?'

'You're wicked. You're trying to find out if I have a girl-friend, or maybe a wife!'

'Absolutely. I'm in a hurry to marry and settle down and have ten children with you.'

'I know. Women say that all they want is to get married, but once they're married they want everything, including a divorce.'

'You must have read the word divorcee on my forehead.'

'No, I read it in your eyes. You must have done well out of this divorce of yours.'

'Maybe it's better if I change the subject and respond to your accusation. Men can't decide whether to get a tattoo or marry a woman with a good figure. My older brother, for example, was in love with a singer who had no voice but was extremely attractive. She sang on television a lot, and after they were married and had lived together for a few weeks, he cursed the day he bought a television.'

'Is that true, or are you being funny?'

'It's a joke. I read it somewhere. Anyway, I haven't asked you what you do for a living, so that I can decide if you're suitable for me or not!'

'I'm a food critic.'

'Fantastic. So I'll never go hungry.'

As if the waiters take this as a signal, they begin covering the tables with dishes of food and opening bottles of wine. James and the others at the table throw themselves eagerly on the dishes and eat ravenously, while she eats slowly and deliberately, like their neighbour Zouzou who was known as the Sipper because he used to take more than twenty mouthfuls to eat a single circle of kibbeh.

'You're pecking at the food like a bird.'

'Oh no, do you think I'm fat?'

'I said like a bird.'

'I heard you. But do you know that birds are very greedy? They either eat or look for food all day long until it's time for bed.'

He collapses into laughter. Luck is on her side again.

'Oh, I like that. You're funny, intelligent, and your dress is wonderful, wonderful.'

'Thank you.'

'Why do you live here and not in Beirut? Ah, how I'd love to visit Beirut. It seems like a fascinating city.'

Before her annoyance can turn into a loss of self-confidence at the idea that he would prefer her to be in Beirut and didn't think how lucky he was to have met her here, she says, 'I prefer living here because I heard with my own ears – before I escaped the war – some fighters in a Christian militia discussing whether it would be possible to kill three hostages with one bullet, by arranging things so that the bullet went right through the first body, then on through the second and third.'

She is indulging him and herself: the war happened years before and now lurks in the dossiers of history.

'I don't blame you at all. The wars of this world are absolute hell.'

What about the wars that families launch against their children for reasons that the children don't understand until they're adults?

Praying Mantis becomes engrossed once more in helping himself to the food and talking about cricket to a man and his wife sitting to his left. When minutes pass, then quarter of an hour and half an hour, without him directing any conversation at her, she stands up and goes over to the newlyweds' table, putting an arm round each of them, and thinks about going outside to talk on her phone, following the analyst's advice for the first time: 'Whenever you feel depressed, call me or someone close to you, or call 123 to listen to the speaking clock, and that will confirm to you that everything changes quickly, nothing stays as it is, and it's the same with relationships. Always remember that men are sometimes embarrassed and shy, or absorbed in their own affairs and totally self-centred. They don't mean to ignore you or humiliate you.'

And you, Madam Yvonne, she addresses herself, *remember that it's only been a few hours since you first met him, so why all the rush and anxiety?*

As she picks up her bag and is about to go out into the courtyard, James calls to her and comes after her: 'Don't say you're leaving!'

'Leave without saying goodbye to you? I wouldn't want you to kill yourself!'

He hugs her delightedly. She likes his body and the way he smells and wishes he would hug her again, and realises that she has also fallen in love with his voice.

He goes into the courtyard with her. 'You're really something else. I haven't asked you what you do.'

If a man had asked her the same question before, she would have been angry with him. *Didn't you ask me that a little while ago? Have you forgotten because you're not interested in what I say, or because you're stupid?*

'I work in advertising, and you're a food critic, so you don't need me and I don't need you, and what brings us together now is this happy occasion and the beauty of the evening.'

'I've drunk a lot. I don't know why I drink more at weddings.'

'You don't seem drunk. You didn't tell me what magazine you write for.'

'It's called *Slow*. It's not as well-known as some of the other magazines, but we have a mission: we're trying to bring people back to home-cooked food.'

'I know it well. Fried ants and roast crickets and grasshoppers. The magazine asked permission, I think it was last year, to publish one of my drawings, and …'

'Tell me you agreed for my sake.'

'For your sake, of course. And you love Lebanese labneh in the shape of little balls like ping pong balls.'

'No! I don't believe it. Is it the drawing of what looks like men's and women's faces and it was hanging in a Lebanese restaurant called Ya Zaman?'

'Ayyam Zaman. Yes, that's mine.'

'I don't believe it. It caught my eye when I went to the restaurant and I liked it. I asked my assistant to contact the artist to ask if we could publish it in the magazine, even though the restaurant assured me that we didn't need permission.'

'That's incredible.'

He looks at her in silence for a few moments before speaking again. 'Since you're the one who drew that picture, you'll be able to understand why I'm so drunk. My wife left me two months ago, but I only found out yesterday.'

'How did that happen? Were you away?'

'No, no. Not at all.'

'So your wife left her twin sister in her place!'

'No, don't rush things. She made me believe that she was still living at home with me, while in fact I was living with a robot that was the spitting image of her.'

She smiles contentedly.

'No, please don't laugh. I'm deadly serious. I was very happy in my marriage until I fell passionately in love with a colleague who came to work at the magazine. To start with, I thought she'd just be like all the other women I'd taken out to dinner in one restaurant or another to try the food, but my love for her became more like an obsession. I asked several of my male friends for advice and in the end I pretended to my wife that I was telling her the story of a friend of mine who had fallen in love with a woman who wasn't his wife and was so confused that he was on the point of leaving his wife and two children to go and live with his colleague.'

'Do you have children?'

'I don't know, but listen to what my wife suggested. Her advice was that my friend should leave home because love doesn't come along that often, and he should follow his heart. This made things even more tangled up than before. My guilty conscience almost killed me because she was completely innocent and totally unaware that I was capable of such treachery. I could no longer sleep or taste food until I thought a waiter in a restaurant had come to my rescue when he asked me to write in the magazine about a robot he had made, as he worked in the daytime in a robot factory in Wandsworth. The robot he'd produced was a waiter like him and it was hard to distinguish it from the human waiter. Of course I let him think I was going to write about this robot of his, and we agreed to meet in the factory. I went early to the appointment and began to cry as I told the robot-maker about my situation and asked him to make me a robot that was the spitting image of me, if he could, so that I could put it in my home to live with my wife who was unaware of what was going on, while I lived with my lover with a clear conscience. The owner of the factory didn't find anything odd about this. He pointed to the dozens of robots around him and said, "All these are exact replicas of real people who've had similar experiences to you and come up with the same solution."

'Before I signed the contract and paid the first install-ment, he looked at me and said, "May I ask why you didn't simply leave your wife, why you're having recourse to a robot?" I answered that in spite of my great desire to live with my colleague I wanted to be sure I had a way back in case I changed my mind after a certain period. We often imagine that we have fallen in love and rush into divorce, only to be disappointed when it's too late and regret is pointless and we've ruined our lives and the lives of those we love, without gaining anything. The man agreed and we arranged that he would contact me when my order was completed. A month later he was in touch and when I entered the factory I was amazed to see a robot exactly like me, sitting there talking and joking with the workers. I clapped a hand over my mouth to suppress a gasp of surprise and admiration and the robot did the same. The manufacturer, my waiter friend, had really done a good job. Even the hair was the same, brown interspersed with a little grey. I was delighted with the result.

"'But what about making love? Does the robot want that?" I asked the man, feeling extremely embarrassed.

"'It can do everything except sex! But I can add a program that will allow it to do that. However, this will take a long time and cost a lot of money. It's a complex program." He paused briefly. "But I deduced from what you said that you stopped sleeping with your wife after you fell in love with another woman."

'Then he went on to explain the other difference between me and the robot, which was a faint ringing sound issuing from one of the robot's ears. Anxiously I asked, "Will this go on all the time? My wife's hearing is as acute as a mole's."

"'Don't worry. Your wife won't hear it unless she puts her ear exactly on top of its right ear. And even if she does that, she'll just think there's something wrong with your ear or the sound is coming from the fridge."

"'I have an idea. Why don't I turn up at home with a hearing aid to make her think that my hearing has got worse recently and that's why I've been so quiet?" I asked.

"'You're one step ahead of me," laughed the robot-maker.

'Then I asked the final question: "But you haven't told me how the robot stops moving and talking."

"'When it's asleep, like us," he answered.

'"No, I meant when I want to dispense with its services. How do I kill it?"

'"By pressing on its right ear. And if you want to reactivate it, you press on the same ear, just like a computer."'

Yvonne quickly moves close to James, putting her ear against his. 'Ah, I can't hear any ringing. You're the original. Come on, now tell me how your wife left you.'

'I won't finish my story until I make sure that you're real and not a robot. Maybe my wife sent you to spy on me.' He puts his mouth on her right ear and she hears the breath escaping his lips. Is he telling her he's married? That's of no consequence to her, for he's attractive and entertaining. Wasn't she on the point of having a relationship with his legs alone?

'Listen, my friend, to what happened the day I decided to leave my wife. I crept out of bed to wait for the robot-maker to come at dawn with my twin in pyjamas like mine. Then all I had to do was press the robot's ear to activate it and it would head off to the bedroom and everything would be fine. But I suddenly remembered I'd left my phone on the table by the bed. When I went back into the bedroom, my wife asked, "What's happened? I heard a lot of noise." "Sorry," I said. "I was in the toilet for ages. I don't know what I ate last night. I've got a bit of a stomach ache so I took something for it." Reluctantly I got back into bed and pretended to go to sleep but as she was restless, I found myself moving close to her and taking her in my arms so that she would go back to sleep, imitating our dog that we lost a year ago, who used to snuggle into one of us to help himself fall asleep. My wife fidgets again. Does she think that because I'm holding her tightly I'm beginning to want to make love to her? I pull her closer to me, afraid she'll get up and go down to the kitchen and see the robot. I breathe into her neck. She fidgets. I rest my face against hers and hear a faint ringing coming from her, or have I imagined it? I start in fear and she asks, "Are you in pain?" "A little," I say. "Let's go to sleep." I tried not to move once I'd taken her in my arms again and held my breath, hoping she would go deeply asleep so that I could make my escape, and there was the ringing once more. I brought my ear close to her right ear and the ringing grew louder. Abruptly I pressed on her ear with all the strength I could summon and the ringing stopped and everything in her stopped. I began shaking her, shouting at her, slapping her cheeks. I tried to open her eyes. It was no use.'

James buries his head in his hands, then looks up and asks Yvonne, 'Did she beat me to it because she had a lover of her own, or did the robot-maker tell her what I was planning? Where is she? I just want to know the truth.'

'But you're free of her, of the responsibility of deciding whether to leave her, and now you can live with your colleague, your lover, without feeling guilty, while your wife is the one chewing her fingernails and maybe regretting what she has done.'

'But I want to know who she's fallen in love with and when it happened.'

Yvonne holds him, comforting him as if he's her child, and says, 'Perhaps your robot and hers could live together. That's the best solution in my opinion. What do you think?'

'But why am I suffering, I wonder? Do I still love her? How can I love someone who's been unfaithful to me? Is it curiosity to find out what happened, or dented self-esteem?'

'But the two of you are even now. Don't forget that you were unfaithful too. Won't you take me to the robot-maker? I want him to make an exact copy of me that can sometimes go to the office in my place. You haven't told me what you did with your robot. Can I hire it? I'd like it to come and live with me.'

He approaches her ear. 'Oh, what a beautiful ringing sound and it smells of perfume too. The name is somewhere in the back of my mind, but I can't recall it now.'

Rather than satisfying her hunger, his sweet talk makes it more acute. 'It's …'

'No, no, let me think carefully. Musk and sandalwood? Or jasmine and amber?'

'It's amber and vanilla.'

'Of course, you're waging chemical warfare to catch men.'

He leans in towards her. As he reaches her lips and touches them with his, a miracle happens: her mind turns into a blank page, the past and the future erased from it. The kiss lasts until they both need to breathe.

'I like this robot's kiss. Is it sparrows' tongues with sumac and thyme?'

'Who cooked that dish for you? Don't say it was my aunt!'

'Of course it was. On my last visit to Lebanon.'

'Did she tell you how she thought of this dish?'

'I didn't ask her. I was too busy eating and looking at her legs. They were fantastic!'

'It was my aunt who invented this recipe on her son's wedding night so that when he was alone with his bride he would deflower her as if he was Samson the Giant and—'

'Who's Samson the Giant? A Lebanese weightlifter?'

'No, he's the Lebanese Minister of Defence who always introduced himself as "the Minister of Boum Boum". The point is that my aunt went out into the fields to catch birds by putting wax on tree branches and scattering almonds and pine nuts and sugar on them so that when the birds came to peck them their little feet would get stuck in the wax and my aunt would hurry to cut out their tongues, then she'd set them free. She prepared such a delicious dish that her son forgot about his bride waiting for him and asked his mother to make him another plate of birds' tongues. The next day the bride came out on to the balcony stretching happily, delighted at the way her wedding night had turned out as her groom had kept going all night long, his resolve never flagging. Suddenly she heard a sparrow talking to her. "You theem happy, you thlut." He looks at her in disgust and another sparrow comes past and says the same thing: "You theem happy, you thlut,' then a third, fourth and fifth, a whole flock of sparrows chanting: "You theem happy, you thlut."'

James laughs, pulls her towards him, laughs some more, kisses her again. The kiss this time feels like a butterfly alighting on a flower, then the butterfly folds its wings and the kiss is more like an iron pressing silk. He kisses her once more and bites her ear. 'Look, I've stopped the robot working. I can take you and do what I want with you.'

Yvonne pulls him towards her, he responds, entwining his legs and thighs with hers, but the appearance of some guests stepping outside to smoke makes Yvonne disentangle herself from the embrace.

She and James go back to their table to find it set with dishes of Iranian food. James and the other guests around the table eat with appetite and obvious enjoyment, while she alone is content to enjoy the smells, like a dog, and furtively observe James's legs.

'And now tell me how you founded your business,' says James eventually.

'I saw a television programme about grouper fish: the females live in rocky caves among coral and seaweed while the males live outside, guarding and protecting them. But if a predator kills the males, a female can change her colour from red to deep purple and become a male, with the ability to fertilise the females. I decided to imitate a grouper: I fertilised myself and worked hard until I had my own business!'

'Did you flee the war with your family?'

'No, Ingmar Bergman whispered to me that I should leave Lebanon.'

'Ingmar Bergman in person!'

'Yes, in person! I was watching a Cypriot television channel. My brother was in a Christian militia and he ran an electric cable from the presidential palace. I'd never seen a film that wasn't American before. The Swedish language began to whisper in my ear as I saw the characters suffering in silence. They complained about their troubles to the clouds and to the sky that hung close to the sea. The pale light in the film, when the only light we had in the pitch black darkness of our town was the gleam of cats' eyes, the whole atmosphere, made me feel comfortable and safe for the first time and forget the war raging in Lebanon, so I thought about going to Sweden.'

'And did you go to Sweden, really?'

'No. I came directly to London with a politician's family from our area in northern Lebanon as a nanny to their daughter, although I was only eighteen. After a couple of years I discovered that I could work and study at the same time, so I registered at an art college. And the rest you're starting to find out.'

'The rest I know, apart from one thing: have you become a female again, or are you still a male like a grouper?'

'Why don't you find out for yourself?'

'I'll try after I've answered the call of nicotine. It's crying out to me.'

She stops herself asking if she can come with him.

James comes back from his cigarette break talking to a dark-haired woman who looks Iranian, with golden skin and kohl-rimmed eyes. *Oh God, don't tell me he likes people who are the opposite of him, when I'm blonde like him.*

They stand there, engrossed in conversation. The woman nods her head. Is he telling her the story of the robot or the sparrows' tongues? They walk a bit and then stop again. Now the woman's probably telling him her life story. They head for the table by the mirror. Yvonne's heart lurches. Is he going to sit with the woman and let someone else sit in his place? 'The bird delouses itself while the hunter is on tenterhooks.' The men in her area used to compare a worried person to a hunter, and the unconcerned object of his anxiety to a bird, calmly picking lice out of its feathers. James returns to his place and everything in her rejoices. Perhaps the Iranian woman was the hunter and James the bird.

'Hi, did you see the woman I was with over there by that table? She reminded me of the woman I used to be in love with.'

'The robot.'

'Exactly.'

'So the robot's real!'

He is silent briefly. 'We split up two years ago. What can I tell you! When we made love it was incredible. Thinking about it drives me crazy.'

'Have you tried to contact her?'

'She did, once, by mistake.'

Yvonne pinches her thigh, tensing the muscles in her bottom automatically, as usual when confronted by a hurtful situation. Her stomach and bottom are focal points for her, like breathing. She feels ashamed of herself now. She'd imagined that the magnetism she felt was based on mutual attraction, but the door has slammed in her face once more.

'Why don't you get back together? Does she still love you too?'

'Love sometimes turns people into monsters. Let's change the subject.'

'It frightens me to think that we have to forget about a person who is so important to us, the oxygen we used to breathe. Cutting such a person out of our lives is like amputating a limb. Aren't we being untrue to ourselves if we do this? How can we turn our backs on such an important period of our lives, imagine that we have to live at a distance from those who have given us profound experiences, even if they involved pain and bitterness?'

He brings her hand up to his mouth and plants dozens of kisses on it. 'You seem to have suffered in love like me.'

She nods in agreement, even though she hasn't been talking about a lover, but about the past and her family and Lebanon. One memory after another, they pound in her head like the thud of the pestle in the mortar that she longs for now to remind her of normal life. These pestles and mortars were made of brass and she used to hear the pounding noises coming from the other houses and wish she lived there instead of in their house. The mothers in the other houses weren't bigheaded like her mother, who had never used a pestle and mortar in her life. She'd even planted basil in theirs, while the other mothers used them to crush garlic and black pepper. Yvonne had lived for seventeen years in that house anchored on the seashore in peace and in war, impervious to the changing seasons; she used to think she too was tied to the place with thick ropes like ships' ropes, but with each visit to Lebanon she found the ropes that bound her had begun to fray, to disintegrate, to dissolve as if they were made of salt.

'Now I want a recipe for a Lebanese dish that I've never tasted or even heard about in my life.'

'How about praying mantis with garlic and cumin?'

'Praying mantis? The green insect with a head like ET? Do you eat them in Lebanon? I suppose you must eat the females to avenge the males. As I'm sure you know, the females eat the males after they've had sex. Are you intending to do that with me tonight?'

'That depends on you.'

If they did spend the night together, she would make him forget his lover; but she wonders if he has invented the whole story.

He kisses her beside her mouth and stands up. He wants a refill and all the bottles ranged along their table are empty.

'Can I top you up?'

'Yes, thank you.'

Is this all a dream? Everything around her has become meaningless. An Iranian couple invite her to dance with them. Perhaps they noticed that she was on her own. She tries to make her excuses; she prevaricates; she doesn't want James to come back and not find her. When she accepts their invitation and joins in the dancing, she keeps her eyes fixed on the table. He hasn't returned. She looks around a few moments later and he is behind her, dancing alone. She rushes over to him and pokes him in the stomach. He opens his eyes, smiles and takes her in his arms. They continue dancing together. She puts her arms round his waist and tells him that Ghulam's relatives insisted she dance with them and that she was afraid he would come back and not find her.

'But I haven't met you before. My name is James. What's yours?'

They embrace and she offers him her lips. It is a long kiss. She has experienced a drought and now the spring is bursting with sweet water again. They disengage their lips in order to drift away into their own worlds. James stays where he is, dancing, his eyes closed; she continues to dance but her eyes never leave him.

She pinches James's hand; he opens his eyes, takes her in his arms and carries on dancing. Everyone is dancing, each person in love with someone they know or a complete stranger, or with the music, or anything else. Love moves around, jumping from person to person, like a bee sipping nectar and dropping pollen; the tighter she holds James, the tighter he holds her.

His eyelids are closed over two turquoises; his voice filters down to her in a whisper, perhaps because he is so tall; it drops gently on to her thumping heart. Enough of all this waiting, or maybe she enjoys tormenting herself! He holds her close even though his eyes are shut. They are the source of her suffering: imprisoned within them is someone other than her. She circles around herself incessantly, like an insect that risks being burnt on the light at any moment. Music is the logic now, reminding her that if she's not in a relationship, it's not because she's possessive or lacking in self-confidence, or because she tries to seduce men with her money, but only because she's never been lucky enough to meet an amazing person like James.

'How old are you?'

'What?'

'How old are you? I haven't asked you how old you are!'

'Thirty-seven.'

'I'm thirty-three.' She subtracts a couple of years. He holds her tight, kissing her near her eyes as if he wants to sip from her skin. He must be tired of bending down to reach her lips. Perhaps he suffers from back pain. She wonders if he has more vertebrae than her.

'James, they're bringing sweets made from Yemeni honey.' No response. 'Yemeni honey has a special aroma. I wonder where Yemeni bees get their nectar. Perhaps from henna flowers ... chestnut henna!'

He carries on dancing, or his legs do. Are they what decide to keep dancing, or is it his mind? She tries again: 'Shall we go back to the table, and have some dessert?'

He doesn't answer her. She'll try again. She's a masochist, yes, a masochist. The conventional definition of masochism is wrong. Masochism is the friend of those who want to make themselves happy, who persist in looking for love rather than being content with despair and regret. Her analyst once shouted at her: 'You prefer other people to yourself. That's a mistake. You have to be number one.' Now Yvonne shouts at the top of her voice, in Arabic: 'When I find my other half, then I'll become one.'

Should she return to the table alone, wait for him until he gets tired of dancing and rejoins her? But before she reaches the table she stops suddenly, rooted to the spot, involuntarily reminded of the tale of the man who promised his neighbour fruit from his date palm and when the tree bore fruit the man went to collect the fruit promised to him and the owner of the palm tree said to him, 'It's better if you wait till the fruit is riper.' When it was riper, he said, 'Leave it until it's soft.' And when it was soft, he said, 'Leave it until the sun has dried it.' When the sun had dried it, the owner of the palm tree went back on his promise and didn't give his neighbour a thing.

She returns to the dance floor and the noise of the music. She stops in front of him; his face is contorted as if he is in pain; he swings his head in all directions, apparently trying to break free of it. She wonders if he is weeping silently. She stands right up close to him and puts her arms around him. When he doesn't hold her or open his eyes, she whispers silently, 'How can you give me something that you don't have?'

She hurries to the table to pick up her bag. A woman guest stops her: 'Your dress is wonderful. You look like a daffodil in it.' Yvonne thanks her and goes on her way.

As she drives away, her last image of him dancing alone stays with her, and will remain stuck in her mind for a long time to come.

She is glad she didn't said goodbye to him, so that if she remembers him one day and remembers the wedding, she'll smile instead of sobbing and lamenting her fate. James was like the man who walked by when she was lying on the sand sunbathing: just for a moment his shadow embraced her, covering her completely.

She has escaped the blaze. She drives quickly now, racing the river that suffers from insomnia because of all the lights gleaming and twinkling from buildings and moored boats. She has everything she needs: stomach, heart, gut, two legs, as well as somewhere to live, a bed and a pillow. Supposing James had agreed to come with her that night, he would have fallen asleep sooner or later while she dozed alone, although at least she would have been in his arms. But even ants can't live on their own. If an ant finds itself alone one day it goes on hunger strike, preferring death to loneliness. It dies within a week, and when the other ants gather round to pay their respects, they smell its excretions and realise it has died of loneliness, and that there was nothing else wrong with it.

Suddenly Yvonne bursts into tears; then she starts laughing. She remembers something her neighbour said to her husband: he had apologised shamefacedly to his wife for farting in her hearing and she had answered, 'Never mind. I'm glad I finally got something out of you.' Yvonne laughs again, uncontrollably. She opens all the windows. The breeze carouses merrily around the car.

A message on the phone. She jumps, praying it's from James so she can turn round and go back to him. It's Huda. *Great, Huda's at home, I won't be alone.*

Yvonne's mobile rings when she's in the lift. Her heart begins to beat, making the lift move at a crazy speed. It isn't James. 'Where are you? Where are you?' says Huda's voice.

'In Malta! I'm in the lift!'

She sees the door of her flat and her throat tightens. When she left home at noon, she was all expectation and enthusiasm, certain that she would meet a man at the wedding and bring him back here – at his insistence of course – so she had tidied the living room and the kitchen before she went out.

Huda rushes towards her and begins to tell her what happened between her and Ta'abbata Sharran, beginning with the demonstration at the American Embassy, continuing with the virginity strawberry and 'I've married you before God and His Prophet', then the trip to the restaurant and how she'd escaped from Hisham's claws.

Yvonne gasped. 'My God, you're so crafty! You could milk an ant, Huda.'

'Oh God, how did I let myself fall into this trap, and I laid it myself. "He who digs a hole for his brother, is the first to fall into it." And who with? A religious fanatic.

And it was as if we were in the Tower of Babel and didn't understand each other's languages.'

'You're a thug!' exclaims Yvonne admiringly. 'But you haven't told me the juicy details.'

'It was a joke. As if he was driving an automatic. Can you believe that for the sake of a few drops of blood, he brought two witnesses?'

'How strange is a person's relationship with his God.' They both start to laugh, then Huda says: 'But what's annoying me is that I was forced to go to your office. I'm sorry, Yvonne, I shouldn't have, but he insisted on coming with me, although I tried my hardest to avoid it, but he still insisted, so I pretended your office was where you lived. So watch out, he might come there tomorrow.'

'You should be afraid for him. I'm going to strangle him with his own shirt collar, pull his trousers so tight he won't be able to breathe. I promise you'll hear the sound of me beating him up wherever you are.' *Even a religious man, obsessed with God and the hereafter, allows Huda into his heart, then goes crazy about her*, thinks Yvonne irritably. *Of course he claims that he wants to please his Lord, but the truth is that he wants to hang on to her by whatever means.*

'Oh Huda!' Yvonne begins to cry.

'What's happened, Yvonne? What's happened?'

'I briefly fell in love, Huda. But he loves someone else. We were at the wedding and the pot found its lid, then I discovered he still loved the woman he'd split up with. Why is bad luck always just around the corner? Did my mother make a pact with the Devil so that every man I like runs away from me?'

'Grow up, Yvonne. If the Devil obeyed your mother's orders, she'd be ruling the world by now!'

'That's true. I never thought of that!'

They laugh and sip wine and it goes to their heads a little and makes their eyelids heavy but then Yvonne jumps to her feet again, sobbing uncontrollably.

She tells the story of her encounter with James, and the warmth and love and longing that had transformed her into a blazing torch at the wedding begin gradually to die away. If someone took an X-ray of her now, it would show how her insides had changed from fiery red to blue, the colour of cold water. 'I don't know what else to do, Huda. I've lost weight; my personality's changed; to put it bluntly, I've become a mouse, and yet I still have no luck!'

The two of them attempt a laugh without success.

'I was offered a drink of water, then it was taken away before I could drink, like the tide ebbing and flowing. Perhaps now I ought to buy sperm and have a child, and forget about men. I should remember what my granny used to say: "Trusting men is like believing you can carry water in a sieve."'

'Yvonne, stop it. Don't make a mountain out of a molehill. He's sure to think about you sooner or later. Who knows, maybe he just happened to remember his ex for a few moments when he saw someone who looked like her at the wedding, and imagined that he still loved her. I remember meeting the mother of one of the Arab actors I worked with in Canada, who told me that she was in love with a singer and heard his voice in her head constantly, even in her sleep. It turned out the singer was Abdel-Halim Hafez. When I told her he'd died more than thirty years before, she answered with tears in her eyes, "I know, I know! But I still love him. He's always with me and I still remember every moment that we were together."'

'No, it's better that I don't hold out any hope. I don't want to go back to being the old Yvonne. Come to think of it, today's been a great success. I've escaped from James by the skin of my teeth and avoided all the sacrifices, the sleepless nights, the wavering between yes and no, and you've managed to have your revenge on Ta'abbata Sharran and said a proper farewell once and for all to your childhood. Absolutely no nostalgia allowed!'

'How did you know what I was thinking?'

'Didn't you know that true friends know each other's thoughts without any need for words?'

'I love people like you who are always ready with a good answer, like a magician producing a dove from his sleeve. And I want to tell you something else. I'm so lucky that my play is going to transfer to London so I'll be able to see you all the time. But you should enjoy the memory of your meeting with James. Let it be a source of happiness for the rest of your life, like the memory of a beautiful dream, rather than a relationship doomed to failure.'

'Do you want me to be like the actor's mother who still wakes up and falls asleep to the voice of Abdel-Halim Hafez? Shall I call the analyst and tell her what happened to me at the wedding? Maybe I did wrong to leave without saying goodbye to him.'

'On the contrary, the way you left was really great. You made it clear that you could do without him.'

'But I don't want James to think that I like playing the field. I want him to know that I was attracted to him.'

'He's not an idiot! He'll know exactly what happened between you. Come on, let's go to sleep. You must be exhausted. I know I am. I want to be absolutely ready for my appointment at the theatre tomorrow morning. Sleep well.'

But Huda finds herself calling Mark in Canada, who is expecting her call even though they haven't planned it.

Hearing his warm, sincere voice makes her regret what she has done with Hisham. *Never mind,* she consoles herself. *Maybe a new play will come out of it, and I'll give the role of Ta'abbata Sharran to my dear actor.*

Yvonne closes her eyes, sending James messages in her head, just as the fortune-teller told her to do: 'Before you go to sleep, you must think of the hummingbird: he never forgets the flower whose nectar he has sipped. So if you send mind-messages to the person who has tasted your kisses, whose body has touched yours, he's sure to come back to you asking for more.'

Yvonne sleeps deeply, unusually for her, and doesn't wake before nine in the morning. So it's true that night can sometimes be heaven if you're trying to escape from something. Suddenly she remembers Huda and rushes to the room next door. When she finds Huda still fast asleep, her eyes fill with tears. *I'm alone,* she muses to herself. *If only I shared this flat with Huda, things would be easier.*

Yvonne dresses quickly. She has to design an advertisement that will catch the eye of all London; she'll make James come crawling after her on his hands and knees. Success is the best revenge.

She attempts to follow the advice of the Lebanese proverb: 'If you have a door that lets in a draught, block it off and forget it.' She takes down a book of Arabic proverbs to cheer herself up. Opening a page at random, she reads: 'If a tree is cut down with an axe, it grows again.' *Great, I like it.* She searches for more sayings: 'Patience is the cure for sorrow'; 'Time is the great healer'. She nods in agreement, but then reads: 'Sex is the cure for love'. She throws the book on the floor, then picks it up again and puts it back in its place.

Yvonne feels comfortable for the first time since the previous day, walking in streets full of people and cars and noise. When she enters her office and sees the posters she has designed over the years covering the walls, her self-confidence increases. The hours pass and although she has an eye constantly on her phone, this doesn't distract her from designing a new poster, inspired by the wedding reception. The subject should be food, to attract James's attention!

The entry-phone buzzes frequently, but suddenly she is aware of her receptionist answering, 'I'm sorry. We don't have anyone here called Huda.'

She rushes to snatch the receiver from him. 'Are you asking about Huda?'

'Yes, Huda,' says the voice of the youth from the desert.

'Just a moment. Wait one moment.'

When he's standing in front of her, all she can see is a tall, incredibly handsome man. *He's the enemy, Yvonne. Remember he's the enemy.* Then she asks him out loud: 'Where's Huda? Please tell me.'

'I've come to ask about her. She's supposed to be staying with you, isn't she?'

'The last time I heard from her was yesterday when she called me while she was with you. We were supposed to meet in my flat but she didn't turn up. I couldn't sleep the whole night. I kept calling her but never got a reply. In the end I convinced myself that she'd forgotten all about me because she was so happy with you and that she—'

He interrupts irritably: 'But I took her to your flat myself yesterday evening.'

'That's odd. I was back home by around nine. God, what's happened to her? We must inform the police.'

'But I saw her with my own eyes tapping in the code and going through this door. She even waved goodbye to me when she was inside. I don't understand.'

'But this is my office, not my flat. It's strange.'

'I understand everything now. She's run away from me.'

'Run away? Why would she run away? What happened? Come on, tell me. But anyway, where would she go? She'd just come home to my flat. I think it's best if we go to a café and talk about things calmly.'

She closes the main door of the building behind her.

'Please tell me what happened,' she says as they walk along together, her face clouded with anxiety.

'I know she called you when she was with me. Did she tell you anything about what was going on between us?'

'She said she'd be late, and that she was having a lovely time with you.'

Yvonne goes into the café close to her office and collapses on to a chair at the first vacant table she comes to. He sits down facing her.

'Tell me, please, does she know anyone apart from you in London?'

'No, I don't think so. She arrived in London on Thursday and hasn't contacted anyone as far as I know.

Now can you please tell me why you think she's run away from you? I'm really worried.'

'Because I asked her to marry me, and it looks as if she doesn't want to marry me, so she's run away.'

'Naturally. Huda would have thought you were insane, if you don't mind me saying so, proposing to her when you'd known her for a few hours. Anyway, she and I decided that we would never get married even if Leonardo DiCaprio proposed to us!'

'Insane! Thanks a lot. Let me explain it to you: the marriage I suggested is a civil marriage, like a common law marriage here, no mosque or state authorities involved, just me and her in front of two witnesses, that's all there is to it.'

'Sorry, but I don't understand why you would want to do that.'

Hisham tells her about the temporary, secret marriage that took place between him and Huda. 'We were married alone, just her and me before God and His Prophet, and we should have registered the marriage in front of two witnesses afterwards. That's all there is to it, but now she's escaped.'

'I don't really understand, or care,' says Yvonne quickly. 'What bothers me now is where Huda is, why she didn't come back to my flat. Let's just suppose that she wanted to get away from you. Would she disappear without contacting me and telling me all about it? Huda knows me well, and she knows that I'd be concerned about her and tell the police.'

She gets to her feet just as the waiter brings two cups of coffee.

'Drink your coffee and I'll go up to my office and let the police know.'

'Please wait for me. Listen, it's clear as day. She was sure you'd think she'd spent the night with me and you wouldn't be anxious before midday today.'

'But how do you explain the fact that she hasn't contacted me? That's what terrifies me.'

'Because she's clever and she knows that I'd turn to you to help me find her.'

'You talk as if she's committed a crime! It seems like you're trying to find her out of your own self-interest rather than because you think she might be in danger.'

'I don't believe she's in any danger! She's a clever girl, very cunning and sly. I've only just discovered that she didn't give me her permanent telephone number, but a temporary UK one that isn't in service, and she didn't even tell me which Canadian state she lived in. Can you tell me which state she's from, please?'

'Canada? I don't believe it! Huda lives in Iceland, in the capital, Reykjavik.'

'Iceland? Is her name really Huda? Huda what?'

'Huda Sukkar.'

'Sukkar? Sugar, like the sugar we eat? You mean her name isn't Huda Kamal?'

'No, Huda Sukkar.'

'And of course she's not a schoolteacher either?'

'She runs a women's refuge in Reykjavik.'

Yvonne buries her head in her hands, rocking to and fro, then gesturing as if she's threatening someone, as if she's talking to someone and unable to believe what she's hearing, then pulling herself together and calming herself down.

'I thought I knew her well. It seems I was wrong. Apparently we don't even know ourselves very well!'

'I want her number in Iceland now, right now.' He takes out his phone. Yvonne searches through her coat pockets: 'Sorry, I've left my phone in the office.'

His face, so full of venom at Speakers' Corner, is bewildered, anxious, and a vein throbs constantly in his temple.

His confusion now, perhaps it's even sadness, spreads to his eyes, and they appear tender, wide, honest and his lips resigned, submissive, waiting for someone to rescue them.

'I should go back to the flat,' continues Yvonne, 'before I call the police, just in case she's come to take her things and return the key. Anyway, here's my number. Call me within the next hour, or I'll call you when I'm back at the flat, and if I don't find her or her clothes, I'll tell the police.'

She turns to talk to the café owner, who appears to know her well: 'I'll send someone to pay.'

They leave the café and before they go their separate ways he entreats her: 'Please tell me if you find her at home, God willing.'

'I will.'

She heads in the direction of her office, turning to make sure he isn't following her. She watches him hurrying away. He's very tall. If he hadn't been so handsome, Huda surely couldn't have forced herself to have sex with him, even as an act of revenge.

When there is no message from James, she finds herself looking on the internet for the sites where she used to chat with other single women.

Not a grain of patience remains inside her. She thinks of contacting James now, but hesitates once again. The best solution would be to look for the Holy Bible she'd inherited from her grandmother and taken everywhere with her since childhood, and swallow one of its pages, like their neighbour in Lebanon who suffered from kidney stones: each time a stone moved and he was attacked by a wave of pain he rushed to the Bible and ate, according to the level of the pain, half a page or a whole page.

*

Huda enters the flat, calling, '*One Thousand and One Nights* will be on the British stage in a couple of months. We'll begin rehearsals in ten days!'

'God must love me,' answers Yvonne at once. 'He wants you to stay in London for my sake.'

A flood of messages arrive from Hisham, which she answers one after the other as they arrive, helped by Huda while they have lunch together in the courtyard at Somerset House. She laughs because he writes her name in English 'Yfonne', using the letter 'f' instead of the foreign 'v'.

'Brother Hisham, Huda came while I was away and took her things and left a note apologising for not saying goodbye to me. She had to leave suddenly for reasons beyond her control. She'll contact me from Iceland in about eighteen months, God willing.' Then Yvonne feels sorry for Hisham and writes 'in a week, God willing' instead.

'Can you give me her number?'

'Sorry, I have to ask her first. The main thing is she's fine. I'll be in touch with you soon.'

'I don't understand why you have to ask her first.'

'She told me not to give you her number. Sorry, my hands are tied. Really sorry.'

'But I have to talk to her.'

'I'll tell her.'

'She knows. Tell her from me, if she's got any sort of a conscience she has to contact me.'

'How are you going to get married in front of two witnesses if she's in Iceland! Are you planning to go there?'

'Certainly not. Please convince her to contact me.'

That night Yvonne escapes with Huda to a Sufi centre in Talgarth Road where would-be Sufis whirl around in the dance of the dervishes to meet their Creator and become one with Him. A member of one of the lonely women's chat rooms described this experience as a temporary solution to feelings of pain and despair.

To begin with, Huda refuses to join the circle of novices with Yvonne, scared that she will burst out laughing, but the rhythm of the music draws her gently in and she thinks to herself if only her parents had whirled around to music at home, alone with God, silent and humble, instead of all the threatening and browbeating and fear.

Yvonne whirls round and round with the others and after numerous attempts stops crashing into people. As she spins she opens her heart wide to chase away grief and let in tranquillity. To help herself focus, she digs into herself like an egg digging a place for itself in the womb in order to become a foetus. She whirls round and round but instead of becoming aware of her Creator she becomes aware of her nipples and instead of becoming one with her Creator she becomes one with James. She falls asleep quickly that night, but wakes up in the morning as if from a terrifying nightmare, and as if everything she achieved the evening before was only a dream, with no basis in reality. When she enters her office, Hisham is waiting for her.

'I can't wait a whole week. I have to contact her today. It's absolutely vital.'

'She hasn't been in touch with me, and I tried to call her but there was no answer.'

'If you don't want to give me her phone number, then what about her email, or is that forbidden too?'

She bursts out laughing. 'Huda and email, you must be joking. Huda hardly knows how to answer her mobile. She refused to let me teach her how to use an iPhone. Listen, brother Hisham, we're in exactly the same boat. I'm suffering just as much as you are. I got to know a man and I thought God had finally made my wishes come true. But he disappeared, melted away like an ice cube. I advise you to accept that you were with her for a day, it was a passing thing and it's over. That's what I did, and I was with my boyfriend for six months.'

She is lying, or perhaps not, if she adds her few hours with James to the two days with Lucio, the weeks with the Lebanese lawyer, those months with the French Moroccan and all the entanglements and infatuations with different men over the years.

'No, please, you misunderstand the situation. This is between me and my Lord and my religion. I want to clear my conscience. Of course you won't understand what I'm saying. That's why I have to talk directly to her. I'll go to any lengths to talk to her. My mind won't rest until I do.'

'But you have to understand that Huda's a modern woman and she doesn't believe in marriage as you've described it to me! I admit she cut short her trip and went back to Iceland because she didn't want to be forced into doing something against her will.'

Hisham converts his hand into a fist and instead of striking the table strikes his forehead, shaking his head as if he wants to deny what he has heard. 'We committed the greatest sin possible. That's why I want to put it right and return to a life of piety. Your friend has plunged me into sin and the only way I can atone for this is by her agreeing to marry me in front of two witnesses. There's no other way.'

Yvonne gets up to fetch coffee and biscuits for him, and asks one of her employees to come to her office in five minutes.

'I'll help you talk to her, be assured of that, and if she refuses I'll give you her number, even if she doesn't want me to.'

He stares at the coffee without attempting to reach for it. When he stands up, the pulsing vein in his temple looks fit to burst.

'Goodbye. Peace be with you,' and he hurries away.

All the same, when Yvonne leaves the office, she dawdles through shops, cafés, underground stations, entering and leaving via different exits, and waits in a bookshop for about half an hour before finally calling a taxi and hurrying home, where Huda is waiting for her.

'How lucky you are, Huda! Hisham is obsessed with you and I don't believe this all just stems from his desire to keep God happy. His love seems to have grown in spite of the disastrous effect my lies had on him.'

'Yvonne, I bet you that in a few days he's going to try and sleep with you!'

'How much?'

'A thousand Canadian dollars!'

'It's a deal. I'd better start practising what to say to him. Is it "*Allahu akbar*, I marry you"? But tell me, Huda, why don't you call him and hear what he has to say? Of course you're supposed to be in Iceland, but just listen to what he says, then either apologise or scream down the phone at him.'

'Yvonne, my dear, you listen to me. It's no use trying to have a dialogue with someone like him. He told me he wanted to save money so he could invest in gold. When I asked him why, he said because gold is mentioned in the Quran!'

'Perhaps I should buy shares in gold and keep an eye on the stock market instead of thinking about James's blonde hair.'

Yvonne stops answering Hisham's phone calls and text messages. She has explained to him time and time again that she can no longer help him by acting as a go-between. She assures him that she is obeying her friend's wishes. She instructs her office to tell Hisham that she has taken some weeks off, in case he asks about her. When Hisham persists in coming to her office, she decides to work from home for another three weeks until Hisham and his name fade away. Huda has, at this point, returned to London with her play's cast and started on the rehearsals of *One Thousand and One Nights* in the Chalk Farm area.

But somehow Hisham manages to appear on Yvonne's doorstep early one evening. He doesn't press the bell, but gives a couple of faint taps on the door. Oblivious, she opens the door. Without even a fleeting glance around him, he says: 'Is there a time difference between Iceland and London? Can you help me contact Huda, please? I've tried to forget about the issues with her, but I can't.'

'First tell me how you managed to find out where I live?'

'I followed you a few times, but didn't manage to get into the building before. This time I pretended I was delivering a prescription from the chemist. I don't understand why she is refusing to talk to me.'

'Nor do I, and it's for the best if I don't,' Yvonne sighs. She doesn't ask him in, but as he keeps staring at the ground, she feels sorry for him and gestures to him to enter the flat. She leaves him in the sitting room and walks into the kitchen.

She pours two glasses of orange juice. She then gets her iPhone and immediately sends Huda an urgent text to contact her.

Returning to the living room, she points to a chair, and sits facing him. He hesitates before sitting down and then says: 'You must be tired. I noticed how much you love walking. I had to stop and catch my breath when I was following you.'

He can't keep his eyes off her iPhone which Yvonne has laid on the table in front of them. She picks it up, punches a few more keys and says: 'I've just sent her a text message.'

'I'm so sorry to be such a nuisance, but Almighty God has guided me to you so you could help me.'

How I wish that God had guided someone else to me so I could be in heaven tonight, she thinks.

She leaves him again after securing the iPhone in her pocket, walks into the kitchen, and pours herself a double vodka which she camouflages with orange juice. As soon as she is back in her seat, he asks 'Nothing?', thinking that Yvonne is looking at her phone to check if there is a message from Huda.

'It's twenty to nine now and she hasn't called.' He shakes his head, the picture of misery.

'Shall we eat something?' she asks him.

'No, I don't want to eat, thank you.'

'You're very modest.'

'I'm very worried.'

'Take a deep breath, go on, five deep breaths.'

All he does is stare at his watch.

She sips her vodka-laced orange juice. Maybe he wants to pray. His tight black jeans, leather jacket and burgundy scarf are completely out of keeping with someone who prays regularly. He looks more like a person who does yoga. He must be around eight years younger than her. His face reminds her of illustrations in children's stories, and Persian miniatures: the eyes are large, like moons, black eyebrows like two swords, and full lips betraying innocence, not lust. She tries to picture him sleeping with Huda.

She gets up and comes back with half a cold roast chicken, tomatoes, lettuce, bread and olives, and puts them all together on the kitchen table. 'Come on, let's eat something.'

'No thanks, I'm not hungry.'

'This chicken's halal. The woman who helps me in the house and cooks for me is a Muslim from Eritrea, and she only buys halal food.'

'I'm not hungry, thank you.'

'I am. Come and sit with me. Don't worry, we can hear the telephone from the kitchen.'

He sits in the chair, bouncing his foot up and down nonstop. She begins eating, then pauses suddenly: 'Maybe you only like eating with other Muslims?'

'What are you talking about!'

He goes over to the sink, washes his hands thoroughly, and then looks around for something to dry them on. She hands him a sheet of kitchen paper and indicates the rubbish bin. Before reaching for the food, he mutters, 'In the Name of God, the Compassionate, the Merciful', then starts very calmly to eat. To her astonishment he breaks the silence: 'They say that sitting around a table helps resolve important issues.'

'I don't think talking to Huda is that important. If I were in your place I wouldn't be thinking about it. It's quite straightforward: you have to recognise whether you matter to the other person or not, even if the truth is painful. They say an hour's pain is better than pain every hour. If Huda cared about you, or even about me, she would have called us back.' She pauses to say to herself, *God help you, Yvonne, you're such a liar. But needs must, and I want to finish with this Huda business tonight.*

'I just want to hear with my own ears her answer to one question, that's all.'

'What question is that?'

'A question.'

He looks at his mobile. 'It's nearly ten o'clock.'

'Do you think in ten or twenty years wristwatches will be obsolete?'

'I've kept you for too long. But you haven't told me how she got a visa and leave to remain in Iceland. We Arabs rarely seek asylum in Iceland.'

'Her brother was a tourist guide in Lebanon. He met some tourists from Iceland and exchanged addresses with them. After a while he contacted them, saying he'd like to visit their country, so they helped him arrange his visit and once he was there he managed to find work and stay there.' Yvonne was actually relating the story of one of her relatives. 'But maybe you are being hard on her. She's running away, you know. Poor thing, I feel sorry for her. She loved this important politician in Iceland for years but he wouldn't marry her and it left her with a complex about the whole idea of marriage and …'

'No, I don't think her relationship with him was what you think. She was a …' but he stops in mid-sentence.

A virgin for ever. Naturally! says Yvonne to herself.

And Hisham reverts to his original nature: suddenly he changes back into Ta'abbata Sharran, tall and imposing, with flashing eyes. He gets up and hurries to the door. 'Peace be upon you.'

To her surprise she hears a faint tap on the door again, only a few minutes after he'd left so abruptly. 'Does religion forbid him to press the bell?' she says in an audible voice that echoes in the emptiness of the flat. Hisham rushes back in without greeting her. 'Sister Yfonne, you have to talk to her.'

She enters Huda's number and when she hears her voice, she passes the phone to him, so he can hear the recorded voice repeating, 'Please leave a message and I'll get back to you as soon as I can. Thanks for calling.'

When he hangs up without leaving a message, she pretends to tap in the number again: 'Hi Huda, this is Yvonne. Where are you hiding? Please call me. It's urgent.' Still holding the phone she rushes into the kitchen and shouts, 'I forgot I had something in the oven,' and deliberately leaves the phone in the kitchen. 'What would you like to drink? Tea?'

'Nothing, thank you.'

He sits there, shifting his gaze from the floor to her, to his fingers, to the bracelets on his arm and back to the floor. She feels a sudden flood of affection and warmth at the sight of this tall figure in her flat, his breathing, his heartbeat, and the silent furniture all around.

'Tell me, brother Hisham,' and she doesn't know what she is going to say, 'where did you get those beautiful bracelets?'

'Why?'

'Because I didn't imagine that religious men like you wore bracelets!'

'Why? Are we any different from the rest of humanity?'

'Sorry, I didn't mean … Can I see them?', reaching out a hand to take one from him.

He purses his lips into a thin line, raps his palm against his thigh, moves restlessly in his seat, touches his bracelets, and instead of taking them off looks at his wristwatch.

'Is it true that the Casbah in Algiers has four hundred and seventy-two steps?' she asks him.

'I haven't counted them, but there are a lot.'

Rather than having someone like James beside her now, exchanging passionate words and kisses with her, she has to put up with the silence of this tormented man.

She has given herself an ultimatum of the two months till her thirty-eighth birthday, not a day more, to try and get into a relationship and have a baby. She will stop obsessing about the fertility app on her phone and go to the sperm clinic. She has been haunted by the red hearts and red flowers of the app; the red flower telling her that she is ovulating and the red heart indicating that she's had sex. Once, she added a red heart next to the red flower, pretending she'd slept with a man, challenging fate. She'll leave for a few days' break. She'll go to Rome, the city that got her back on her feet after what Lucio did to her. To confirm that she likes herself, she'll eat gelati and sleep soundly. Or maybe she'll visit the Casbah in the Algerian capital and climb up and down the four hundred and seventy-two steps. At Christmas she'll go to Lebanon and volunteer to help refugee children from Syria. Who knows, maybe she'll adopt a child! And she'll see her family in the north of the country for two or three days. Strange, how her mother has never thought of visiting her during all these years, not to mention her brothers or her sister. They must be scared of her.

She pretends to call Huda again. 'Huda, we're waiting for you. Please call back at once.'

'Swear on your mother and father that you and Huda aren't using a secret code.'

'I swear on the life of the Pope and the Virgin Mary that Huda and I aren't using a secret code.'

'Why don't you swear on your mother and father's life?'

'Because I love my father more than *immi*, but he's dead.'

'Swear on your mother's life anyway.'

'I swear on *immi*'s life that Huda and I aren't using a secret code.'

She laughs. He's like a child. She feels as if she is still playing with her classmates at school in Lebanon. *On the Virgin's life, on my mother's life, on the Pope's life.*

'*Immi?* What kind of a word is that? Are you sure it means mother?'

She laughs again. 'That's what we say in Lebanon. How do you pronounce it in Algeria?'

'Would you give me her number, please?'

'Of course.' Assuming a casual air, she gives him the number of her hairdresser, which she has had ready since the first day, for just this kind of situation. 'It's odd that you didn't ask me to swear on the life of the Virgin Mary even though you Muslims believe in her. She's the only woman mentioned in the Quran, isn't she?'

'Who told you that?'

'Huda. Who else? Our Lady, the Virgin Mary, was a kind of mother to me. I hung a little statue of her above my bed. Whenever I got bad marks at school, I asked her forgiveness, promising her that I would work hard just for her sake. And every time I went home after a date with a boy called Jamil, and I was all red from so much kissing, I wasn't embarrassed or afraid of anyone or anything except the statue of the Virgin Mary that was no more than twenty centimetres high. I used to imagine the mother of Jesus looking at me with her innocent, sad, pure white face and her head cover, blue as the waves of the sea, and I would whisper to her, "Forgive me, our Lady. You understand me. You are the source of love, and I love Jamil and feel sorry for him. He has no mother." Then I would lie and say, "When we grow up, we are going to get married and you will be our *shabina*."'

'"*Shabina*"? Is that an Arabic word?'

'Yes. A *shabina* means a witness for Christians in Lebanon. When people get married the bride has a *shabina* and the bridegroom a *shabin*.'

She stands up and fetches the phone and looks at the screen. 'No, Huda hasn't called yet. Would you like some fresh lemonade? I squeezed the lemons a little while ago, and I'll add some orange flower water.'

She repeats in a low voice, 'Jamil, oh Jamil,' as she adds the finishing touches to the lemonade. She puts it down in front of Hisham and returns to her place by the window and sits looking out at the night as if it reflects her own gloom. She sits waiting for Jamil to appear. She smiles as if she hears someone knocking at the door and entering. There is somebody who wants her – it's Jamil and he's come from Lebanon. She is definitely crazy! But isn't it enough that we love something and think about it and imagine that it is happening? The last time she saw Jamil in Lebanon, he hurried away, not wanting her to see him with his bucket and net coming from the sea. Jamil was a fisherman. He must have said to himself when he saw her, 'Poor me living here, and lucky her living in England.'

'Jamil,' she says to Hisham, 'it didn't bother him that I had sturdy thighs and a big bottom. I remember he pinched my stomach once and said, "Come on, what a stomach! I can't wait for you to get pregnant from me when I'm a bit older!" That's love. Love has to be blind. Love is the important thing, and not the shape of the body. My mother's beauty and her figure when she was young were, according to my father, "her power and glory".'

Hisham fidgets uneasily, his hand drumming on his thigh. 'I'll be on my way.'

'Go on, go. Hurry up. I don't want you to sully your faith by listening to me. Why is it that all religious people are afraid to hear what goes on in real life? I remember when I told the priest that I hated my mother and wished she would die, he was taken aback. I was fourteen. But do you know what our father the priest said to me at the door of his church, without having any kind of discussion with me, "Grow up, little girl. Go home. No mother hates her children." I told him she'd hit me because I'd eaten the strawberries she'd brought home specially for my brothers and I was cross with her because she liked my brothers better than me. He repeated, "There isn't a mother in the whole world who prefers one of her children to another. They were all formed in the same womb, my daughter." "I'm sure," I said to him, "that she prefers boys to girls." I began to cry loudly and he ordered me to go home at once and repent and pray and say five Our Fathers and five Hail Marys. Not knowing what I was doing, I found myself shouting at him and threatening to stop coming to church.'

She sees that Hisham isn't reacting to her story and is continuing to shift restlessly in his seat because Huda hasn't called. 'Sorry, sorry, I talk too much, but I'm lonely, really lonely. The laws of nature have decreed that a woman has to choose between being a wife and mother or having a job if she wants to be successful, and I'm successful in my job!'

She looks at him in case he might offer a word of consolation, but he just jiggles his foot up and down more violently.

'And you, I wonder who you love more: your mother or your father? They must have loved you more than your sisters. Arabs always prefer males to females, even though it's the girls who usually stay close to their families.'

'I've taken up too much of your time. I'll leave now.'

'Of course you will.' She gets up to see him out. 'Sorry about Huda's behaviour. Goodbye.'

But he doesn't move from his place and to her astonishment she hears him speak. 'When did you come to London?'

'Over twenty years ago. When I was seventeen.'

'How? Did you escape from Lebanon?'

'No, I didn't escape.'

'Your family allowed you to go abroad?'

'Yes.'

'So your mother loves you, otherwise she would have forbidden you to leave.'

'Actually, she didn't love me, and that's why she let me leave. OK and what about you, how did you end up in London?'

'I left Algeria for France when I was seventeen but I hated it and came here. The French hate Algerians and despise Muslims.'

'So you turned to religion here!'

'Yes, here. My mother was a believer. She was really committed and prayed and fasted constantly, unlike my father. But thanks to me, he became a muezzin in our local mosque. I'm the one who planted the seeds of religion in him a few years ago.'

'I like that,' she laughs. 'It's nice that you influenced your father instead of the other way round. That's much better. It seems he trusts you so he listened to what you had to say and agreed with you. Shall we eat some cake?'

'No thanks.' He places a hand on his chest in a gesture of gratitude.

'I'll bring you some more lemonade then.'

She hurries to the kitchen, pours herself a vodka and orange and takes a few gulps, then goes back to him with lemonade and a chocolate cake.

She is surprised by her sudden burst of mental activity and hurries over to the table to fetch a drawing she made the night before. She lays it down in front of him.

'Tell me what you see.'

Hisham looks at the sheet of paper without commenting, but makes a face, then looks at her as if to say, 'What's got into you, you madwoman?'

'This is an ant and this is a cockroach,' she says.

'I know what they are, but I don't understand why they're important.'

'Because the ant catches the cockroach and drags it alive to her nest to lay her eggs on it. Then the larvae feed on the insides of the cockroach until all that's left is its outer shell.'

Hisham stares at her, the furrow between his eyebrows growing deeper the more he scowls and frowns at her.

'Don't you believe me?'

'I don't know what you're getting at. And the cockroach is disgusting.'

'The main thing now is what you infer from this drawing, what you learn from it. Didn't you wonder, for example, how a tiny ant defeated an insect that was much bigger and stronger?'

'Glory to Him who created it and taught it and granted it strength. Of course I see this divine miracle, but what I don't understand is why you chose this miracle in particular when there are much stranger miracles that God produced in creatures more beautiful than this repulsive cockroach. God forgive me, I take that back. They are all God's creatures and every one of them is useful in its own way.'

'The truth is that I chose the ant and the cockroach to tell young people that they should say no to drugs and not experiment even with a tiny amount, the size of an ant, because it will defeat them like the ant defeated the cockroach.'

'Have you tried drugs?'

'Me? Of course!' She hurries to reassure him when she sees the signs of panic on his face. 'Of course not. This

216

poster will be displayed in schools and trains and a lot of other places.'

She catches him looking at his watch again.

'Sorry, I've talked too much. Shall I try calling her?'

'No, no.'

She gets up and opens the cupboard and returns with an envelope containing photos of her and Huda in Italy, and of her with Lucio. He glances quickly at the first photo – Huda and her in bikinis – and puts it face down on the table. Yvonne remembers the day the photos were taken. She had asked Huda, 'How can I become slim like you?' and Huda had replied, 'I can't tell you, just as you can't tell me how I can be confident and attractive like you.'

'Do you think if your mother was still alive she would have liked Huda, or preferred me because I'm fair and my eyes are green?'

At first he says nothing, but puts a hand over his mouth to hide a smile. Then he says, 'Your questions are very strange, and embarrassing too.'

'How did you marry Huda in secret? Did the two of you read from the Quran and that was enough?'

'Why do you want to know?'

'I'm curious, that's my nature. Unless it's a secret you don't want to reveal!'

'We exchanged this sentence: "I have married you before God and His Prophet."'

'So now you've married me!' she says, laughing.

'No I haven't, because you didn't repeat the same sentence back to me. I have to go now. Peace be upon you.'

'What do you want me to say to Huda if she calls?'

'Nothing. Peace be upon you.'

As soon as she sees him descending the staircase through the spyhole in the door, she rushes to the phone: 'God,

Huda, such a bizarre meeting with Ta'abbata Sharran. Do call me back. From Iceland!'

Once again, there's a faint tap on the door. She hurries to look through the spyhole to check who it is. As expected, it's Hisham. *I'm not going to open to him. He must have tried to contact Huda in Iceland and has come back to tell me off for giving him the wrong number.*

But she opens the door as his knocking grows louder. She smiles to overcome her confusion and prepares an answer in case he begins to reproach her.

'Sorry to bother you. I wanted to talk to you.'

'That's fine, don't worry.'

'The truth is that since I left I've been thinking about you. I mean about your relationship with your mother and your feelings towards her. I wanted to advise you to reconcile with her and stop harbouring a grudge towards her. For as the Prophet said, "Paradise lies at our mothers' feet and the main gate of heaven is reserved for children who have taken care of their parents."'

'You're right. I might think about visiting Lebanon in the very near future.'

She is astonished to see him undoing one of his bracelets and handing it to her. She takes it from him.

'Why are we standing at the door? Please, come in. Oh, this bracelet's heavier than I expected.'

'It was my mother's anklet. She always wore it round her leg.'

'It's so beautiful. Your mother must have been slim.'

'Slim and tall, God rest her soul.'

She notices him muttering something and keeps silent. Maybe he is reciting the Fatiha for his mother's soul. When he's finished, she hands him the anklet and he clasps it and her hand at the same time and then suddenly embraces her. She closes her eyes, happy at this warmth that is so completely unexpected. Long legs, beautiful white teeth. Most likely he never eats sweets and he certainly doesn't drink wine. She is aware of his sex, hard against her, and she fidgets, trying to disengage herself. She doesn't want to have a weird temporary marriage with him.

His embrace is his way of laying the trap and she doesn't intend to fall into it. She feels his sex again and remains silent and unmoving, enfolded by his brown limbs. This is Yvonne, who used to surprise men by taking the first step. Now she's waiting for the right moment to make her escape, as soon as she hears him saying, 'I have married you before God and His Prophet', and asking her to repeat his words. She will protest that she doesn't know the rules of Arabic grammar and will make mistakes with the vowels and the case endings, and if he answers that this doesn't matter, she'll ask him if God knows Arabic grammar well, then he'll lose his temper and change his mind about sleeping with her. Or would it be best to be completely honest and say, 'No, I'm not a Muslim and I don't believe that we have to repeat this formula before we make love'. Or 'Actually I've got my period. Sorry'. Or 'I don't fancy you', or 'I'm engaged', or 'I don't want to marry the husband of my dearest friend'.

But he says not a word, and instead she hears him panting with desire. He's the ant and she's the cockroach and he is trying to immobilise her so that he can suck the nourishment from inside her, and meanwhile his body stops her brain functioning.

They begin to embrace again, then she stops him once more, to take off her skirt and to make sure that she hasn't lost her sense of hearing and that he really didn't repeat that phrase to her. She isn't afraid. She says nothing, but closes her eyes while the thoughts go spinning around in her head. *Now does he think that by having sex with me, he will somehow get through to Huda?*

'Are you going to marry me and make me marry you!'

When he doesn't reply, she says, 'Now I understand. Secret marriage can only take place between two Muslims.'

When his only response is to pull her towards him, she answers him with a kiss on his shy lips, trying to transfer even just a little of the warmth of his body to them, before abruptly moving him off her.

'By the way, are you going to tell me what you want to ask Huda?'

'If she'll agree for us to marry on Skype in front of two witnesses, then after the legal three-month wait I'll divorce her on Skype too. That's what the imam told me to do.'

She takes him by the hand and leads him into her home's pink trap. The curtains are just threads of silk hanging to the floor. The patterns on the wall are her own design and they are like flowing locks of hair without beginning or end. The lights are low, reflecting on the dressing-table mirror, the coloured glass flowers, the Lebanese Tabbara calendar she bought in Edgware Road and the statue of the Virgin Mary that has been with her since she was a child, placed next to the mirror so she would see it every morning when she woke up and every night as she went to sleep. When this bedroom of hers receives not even a passing glance from Hisham, she knows for certain that he is like the men in her family, because usually anyone who came into the room remarked how strange and special it was.

She leads the way to her bed. When he falls on top of her, she whispers to him to take off his trousers and he obeys her, almost losing control of himself in his excitement. She is totally ready to make love and begins to feel waves of intense pleasure, and when he finally withdraws from her and collapses on to her stomach, she smiles to herself – this is the starting line, and she will eventually reach her goal, adding the red heart to the red flower, for real this time. He drifts off to sleep for a few moments, she guesses with a smile on his lips. Then he starts, as if waking from a deep slumber, and looks at his watch. 'There is no power or strength save in Almighty God. What's happened to me? I haven't even washed or prayed. I have to rush to work. Shall we meet tomorrow?'

'Why not?'

'Until tomorrow, then. I'll call you anyway.'

She waits until she hears him going down in the lift before she leaps over to the phone and calls Huda and describes in detail what has just happened between her and Hisham. 'I'm so happy we didn't agree on a price when you bet me that Ta'abbata Sharran would try and sleep with me!'

'But we did. One thousand Canadian dollars, you cheat. But I'll accept sterling since I'm here! See you on Thursday as we agreed.'

Yvonne goes back into her bedroom. She pulls the sheets off the bed and winks at the statue of the Virgin Mary. 'Until tomorrow, then.'

A NOTE ABOUT THE AUTHOR

Hanan Al-Shaykh is one of the Arab world's most acclaimed writers. She was born in Lebanon and brought up in Beirut, before going to Cairo to receive her education. She was a successful journalist in Beirut, then later lived in the Arabian Gulf, before moving to London. She is the author of the short story collection *I Sweep the Sun off Rooftops* and her novels include *The Story of Zahra, Women of Sand and Myrrh, Beirut Blues, Only in London,* and *The Locust and the Bird,* a memoir of her mother's life. Most recently she published *One Thousand and One Nights,* her acclaimed reimagining of Arabic folktales. She has also written two plays, *Dark Afternoon* and *Paper Husband.* Her work has been translated into 28 languages. Hanan Al-Shaykh lives in London.

A NOTE ABOUT THE TRANSLATOR

Catherine Cobham is a lecturer in Arabic and head of the Department of Arabic and Persian at the University of St Andrews. She has translated a number of contemporary authors from Arabic, including Naguib Mahfouz, Mahmoud Darwish, Hanan al-Shaykh, Fuad al-Takarli and Ghayath Almadhoun. She has written many articles in academic journals and co-written with Fabio Caiani *The Iraqi Novel: Key Writers, Key Texts*.